PRAISE FOR CHRIS D.'S NOVEL **TIGHTROPE ON FIRE**

*"Chris D. has staked his claim on the modern Southwestern noir territory, a big, sun-scorched claim. Frankie Powers is a brutal anti-anti-heroine whose code of honor arrives too late with too little. TIGHTROPE ON FIRE hits you where it hurts."*

– Craig Clevenger, author of
the novels THE CONTORTIONIST'S HANDBOOK
and DERMAPHORIA

PRAISE FOR CHRIS D.'S NOVEL **MOTHER'S WORRY**

*"Next time you're set on stealing some cash and a car and bombing your blood-soaked way across Mexico in a barrage of bullets, bitches and badasses – just read MOTHER'S WORRY instead. You'll get the same adrenaline rush, minus the jail time."*

– Eddie Muller, author of
DARK CITY DAMES,
DARK CITY: THE LOST WORLD OF FILM NOIR,
and the novels THE DISTANCE and SHADOW BOXER

*"MOTHER'S WORRY swaps midnight for high noon; Chris D. burns down the speakeasy and pool hall and drags the roman noir across the desert dirt beneath an unforgiving sun. This is my kind of crime novel."*

– Craig Clevenger

PRAISE FOR CHRIS D.'S **DRAGON WHEEL SPLENDOR**
AND OTHER LOVE STORIES OF VIOLENCE AND DREAD

*"Every story delivers a gut punch...Chris D. writes with a clarity so merci-less, reality itself seems to shimmer with menace... His sentences evoke the dark truths of a David Goodis and the savage humanity of a 21st century Dostoyevsky or Zola. Already a cult icon, with DRAGON WHEEL SPLENDOR the great Chris D. should finally find the audience he deserves. This is a book that can kill the voices in your head – or make you love them."*

– Jerry Stahl, author of
PLAINCLOTHES NAKED, PAINKILLERS
and PERMANENT MIDNIGHT

"Chris D. is someone who takes his dreams seriously, for, as Delmore Schwartz said, In Dreams Begin Responsibilities. To that end, Chris D.'s Los Angeles of the mind is awash with a heady mix of forlorn delirium, nostalgia pangs, seductive ghosts, and dangerous desires."

– Grace Krilanovich, author of
THE ORANGE EATS CREEPS

PRAISE FOR CHRIS D.'S NOVEL **SHALLOW WATER**

"One sinister serpent of a story, an old Republic Pictures western serial scripted by James M. Cain and reimagined by Sam Peckinpah. I loved it. Dive in and wallow in SHALLOW WATER."

– Eddie Muller

PRAISE FOR CHRIS D.'S NOVEL **NO EVIL STAR**

"A healthy authorial sense of curiosity and generosity lends weight to NO EVIL STAR's intersecting lives, where Chris D. ably traces out the contours of human torment in a manner recalling American films of the 1970s."

– Grace Krilanovich

"Chris D. has performed in his own bands, directed his own movie and written books, from Japanese film studies to volumes of his own poetry. Now he has written a crime novel, just another facet of the multi-faceted inside of his head. Some people can do one thing – Chris can do almost anything."

– Mary Woronov, author of
SWIMMING UNDERGROUND,
NIAGARA, BLIND LOVE and SNAKE

WHAT WRITERS HAD TO SAY ABOUT CHRIS D.'S ANTHOLOGY
**A MINUTE TO PRAY, A SECOND TO DIE**

"Reading Chris D's blood-on-the-page prose is like running naked, screaming with terror and desire, through the fetid back alleys of American pulp culture. You're seduced, fucked over, doused with whiskey, set on fire, dragged by the getaway car, nailed by the hail from a 30.06 and still, still – you can't stop reading."

– Eddie Muller, author of
DARK CITY DAMES, THE ART OF NOIR and
the novels, THE DISTANCE and SHADOW BOXER

*"...he continues a tradition in writing that is all but lost; authors who use their powers of imagination and creativity rather than simply recounting or inventing a memoir. Like the outsider artists that Chris D. champions, he writes for the future, for art, to someday be truly discovered for the great talent he is."*

– John Doe, singer/songwriter
of X and THE KNITTERS

*"Chris D. presents...such an immense encapsulation of his life's work that it reads as literary autopsy of a man not yet dead but of one who has died a thousand times and somehow miraculously between crucifixions used pen as shovel to prevent himself from being buried alive."*

– Lydia Lunch, musician and author of
PARADOXIA and WILL WORK FOR DRUGS

*"To my mind, the lyrics he wrote...are as blinding a display of raw, universe-gobbling intelligence as have ever been penned...The sources from which Chris drew his inspiration are a classic pop cultural blend – exploitation films of all stripes, pulp fiction, French decadent poets, hot rod gangs, mystical Catholicism, underground biker comix, beatnik booze into the hippie acid continuum, and on and on and on. This is a mix that has gained great subterranean currency over the past few decades, but when Chris was churning through these waters, they were as yet uncharted. His written work (along with that of fellow travelers such as Exene Cervenka, Dave Alvin John Doe and Claude 'Kickboy' Bessy) created a new, totally crazed hipster aesthetic that rejected punk orthodoxy in favor of something much more magnificent and inclusive."*

– Byron Coley, writer for WIRE Magazine,
author of C'EST LA GUERRE:
EARLY WRITINGS 1978-1983
and co-author (with Thurston Moore)
of NO WAVE: POST-PUNK.
UNDERGROUND.NEW YORK. 1976-1980.

# VOLCANO GIRLS

# VOLCANO GIRLS

## BY

## CHRIS D.

A POISON FANG BOOK

*If you enjoy this book, tell someone about it*

A Poison Fang Book

Original screenplay © 1985, 2000 by Chris Desjardins, pka Chris D.

Novel © 2009, 2013 by Chris Desjardins, pka Chris D.

Front and back cover designs by C. D.

ISBN: 0615818803

First Poison Fang Books Edition, October 2013

Printed in the United States

10 9 8 7 6 5 4 3 2 1

For all the original Volcano Girls...

*Devil's River, CA. 1985*

# 1

Merle Chambers, a scruffy, unshaven man of about forty with slick hair, cruel eyes, clad in jeans and a torn suitcoat took a swig from an almost-gone pint of bourbon. He then tossed the pickaxe in the bed of his grimy pickup. He squinted against the blurry glare of the sun that was trying to make some headway through the dawn mist. A cawing sounded just above, and Merle looked up, surprised to see a huge raven sitting on the desiccated branch of the dead oak tree. It blinked down at him, unafraid, and Merle got ticked off as the damned bird got louder. He heaved the now empty bottle at it, and it took wing. its earsplitting cry making him see red.

It was exactly 6:00 AM by the clock on the truck dash. Nothing short of miraculous since the truck was 25-years-old. A 1960 Dodge, and, for all Merle knew, the clock had never stopped working in all that time. He smiled as he thought about it. Evidence of his rock-steady nerves, considering what was about to happen.

He climbed in and slammed the door a couple of times until the lock catch caught and stayed shut. The motor spluttered and coughed as he turned the ignition key, and he pushed in the clutch, shifted into first and took off from the dirt shoulder, swerving onto the asphalt.

He rubbed the greasy palm of his thick, calloused hand across the even greasier, fogged-up windshield. Visibility slightly improved as the opaque moisture smeared. There wasn't a car to be seen anywhere else on the road. Strange, he thought, these hick farmers were usually still plenty industrious, darting around before the sun was even up, despite Devil's River's dying-on-the-vine condition. Get those goddamn vegetables and fruit – or whatever the hell they grew – to market, no matter if it was only for pennies. But where were they today? Fuck 'em. He was glad they weren't around and didn't give a damn why.

What he was headed for wasn't Fort Knox by a long shot, but it was for more than pennies.

Merle slowed down as he caught sight of the black-and-white rolling out of Danny's U-Totem parking lot. There was only one cop in the car, and he was talking on his radio. He didn't even glance over at Merle as they passed each other. Merle felt the Dodge's non-existent shocks as bald tires thumped over the high lip of the parking lot's driveway. He tried to be casual, but he almost dislocated his neck as he snapped round to catch the patrol car disappearing in the morning fog.

He pulled into the center space, the one meant for the handicapped, then rammed the gear into park. He stared through the huge, plate glass doors, trying to search the whole place from where he sat before he made another move. Nobody in sight. He couldn't even spot Sid Fromkiss, the husky, pimply quarterback from St. Dominic's High who pulled the graveyard shift on Thursday nights/ Friday mornings. Probably in the can with one of the tit mags they kept behind the counter. Without letting the storefront out of his sight, Merle reached behind him, grabbed the splintery stock of the sawed-off shotgun from in back of the seat and, in one continuous slick, slippery motion, eased open the door and out of the cab. He left the engine running. It was surprisingly quiet, especially since it hadn't had enough time to warm up.

Coming through the door, Merle smirked. What a rinky dink fucking lameass little place. No one was stirring. Then he heard the kid sawing logs. He took a few more steps, and there was the husky oaf, Sid, his arms folded and crossed on the counter with his head cozily resting on them. Merle nudged the barrel up against the slumbering clerk's mouth. Slowly he worked it between his lips, and the kid squirmed in uncomfortable dream reverie.

Suddenly his eyes shot open.

"The register. Open it."

The kid began shivering with fear. "But-but-but there's only twenty-five dollars change in there!"

"What about that?" Merle gestured at the strange, space-age cash deposit safe embedded and protruding from the floor. He'd seen it spew out plastic cylinders of cash before when the clerk needed change.

"No way. I don't got no key, no combination, no nothin' to open that. Especially me on all-night shift. It just spits out change in bills like, you know, ones, fives, tens and twenties. It'll shut down if I take out too much. You know, if I keep making the machine spit 'em out."

Merle was getting very impatient. "Open the goddamn register."

The kid rapidly responded.

Paranoid Merle grew suspicious. "Now wait a minute, buddy boy, you using both hands there. I know this place well enough, you only need one."

Merle sank to his knees and saw the clerk's other hand fumbling frantically, inches away from an alarm button. With a nasty smile and not even a second's hesitation, Merle squeezed the trigger from his crouching position. The roaring blast was deafening. Sid's head evaporated in an aerosol shower of blood, flesh, bone and brains. The body flopped to the linoleum, scraggly ends of torn arteries shooting convulsive jets of blood on the adult mags displayed in a metal rack next to a battery display. Merle contemplated the carnage. He had heard the word viscera one time at the institution and looked the word up later. Yeah, this is what he would sure enough have to describe as a "visceral panorama," if ever there was one. He smiled at his own grotesque sick humor: "That's the way the quarterback crumbles." Suddenly he remembered why he'd just splattered Sid all over the cigarettes. There was a silent alarm going off somewhere, undoubtedly at the Sheriff's substation. He reached over and grabbed the available cash out of the register, then ran out of the store.

Merle yanked the pickaxe out of the truck bed and raced back inside, leaping the counter and landing on the edge of a slowly growing pool of blood. Smiling, Merle spit in both hands, hoisted the pick, then leveled and aimed, finally slamming it into one corner of the cash dispenser. Immediately audible alarms went off. But Merle's caveman approach produced results. He had hit the machine right at the join of the high tensile seams, and it cracked. Rolled-up bills of various denominations began to shoot out of their respective tubes. Laughing, Merle swept the money away with a maniacal frenzy. He grabbed fistfuls of cash, stuffing it in every pocket, grabbing plastic bags and filling them, too. Knowing instinctively he was taking too long, he started to rush out, then paused, realizing he was forgetting something very important. He ducked into the back room, spotted the VCR next to a food-stained microwave and quickly ejected the video surveillance tape. He tossed it in the cube-shaped oven, shut it and cranked the cooking temperature onto high. The machine was still belching out long green as he bolted from the store.

Right on cue, Merle heard the first siren in the distance. Morons. They must not want to catch me very bad, he thought. Any cop with a half a brain would have left them off. Revving the engine, he stuffed the heavy duty trash bag of cash under the seat, rammed the shift into reverse, jerked the truck backwards, then smashed the stick again into first, second and third in a matter of seconds.

He headed back down the way he'd come, back in the direction of the black-and-white cruiser. It was a risky thing to do, to say the least, but chancy, stupid things were Merle's meat.

His foot was like a piece of concrete weighing on the accelerator. Just before the raging, screaming black-and-white whipped into view, he hurtled the truck down a dirt road shortcut. It had rained the night before, so only mud churned and spiraled into the air. Merle edged it off track into an orange grove between two, widely spaced rows of trees.

## 2

Mona was 37-years-old, but she thought the face that stared back at her from the bathroom mirror looked ten years older. "My face is going to fucking hell," she thought, "losing what's left of my looks." Most of the men who'd had a chance to get close to her – all of whom she despised – would not have agreed. They were still after her, and she was sick of it. She was blind to the smoothly honed, yet delicate, aquiline face, the lustrous thick black hair, features that had only become more individual and attractively pronounced with the passing years, the complex beauty that her half-Mexican, half-Danish genes had given her, the firm, mature suppleness of her body. She examined the faded tattoos across her shoulders and upper arms. She had started on an attempt to remove them but had run out of money for the process, run out of time to journey down to Los Angeles to complete it. Periwinkles. Why had she gotten tattoos of flowers? And periwinkles? So lame. She berated herself, then abruptly softened towards that girl so long ago, barely 25 – long ago, before dreams were crushed. She'd gone down to Oxnard with the boy she loved, a boy who'd been a year before her in college. He'd just graduated, was going in the Army, probably off to 'Nam, though the war seemed to be drawing to a close, and they were celebrating, both getting tattoos.

Now in the 1980s, tattoos were more common, especially among young people. Musicians and city kids were starting to get them. But back in the early-to-mid 1970s, the radical cultural shift hadn't yet taken hold. It was more unusual and rebellious. Her father had still been alive, and he hadn't noticed for weeks because of the long-sleeved clothes she wore. Then the summer had gotten too hot, and she'd said "Fuck it!", wearing T-shirts with the sleeves torn off. He'd exploded when he saw them and, speechless with rage, had knocked her halfway across the kitchen. Her mother, Consuela, had gotten between them.

Six months later, while she was at UCSB, she'd gotten the letter from her boyfriend's mother. He wouldn't be coming back, ever.

She buttoned up the lame pantsuit, her fifth-grade teacher attire – at least it covered up her tattoos – and dragged a brush through her mane of unruly locks. The bristles caught, she yanked the thing and her hold slipped. She hit the various jars and cans of creams, make-up and hairspray that she and her sister Terri, shared. Then there were the empty beer cans, cigarette butts, fashion magazines, comic books, candy wrappers, toothbrushes, razors and paper cups. A couple of cold cream jars clattered to the linoleum, and a little compact mirror broke. Her temper frayed threadbare, Mona swept the whole mess onto the floor in front of the bathtub with a resounding crash. Most of the godawful mess was Terri's. Mona had refused to clean it up anymore, but it had made no difference to her sister. She thrived in squalor.

Mona clenched her fists and closed her eyes. She silently counted to ten, then slowly opened her lids. She straightened her suit outfit then tugged open the door and stormed down the hall into the kitchen.

Gingerly, she took the coffee pot off the stove and poured herself a cup, sipped at the inky blackness, wincing at the near boiling liquid.

"Mona...Mona..."

Mona stepped into the hall, hesitated before her mother's door saying a silent prayer, then bravely entered.

Consuela lay in ornate disarray on the narrow single bed with the massive mahogany frame. As always, Mona found her eyes going straight to the perverse Old World Spanish carvings that dotted the varnished wood.

"Are you all right, dear? What was the noise?"

"Nothing, Mama. Some stuff in the bathroom fell on the floor. I'll leave a note for Terri to clean it up."

"I can do it, Mona."

Mona had to restrain her anger. Her patience for this all to predictable maternal behavior was strained past the breaking point.

"It's okay, Mama. Leave it be. Everything's okay."

"Are you sure, dear? You seem upset."

"Yes, I'm sure, Mama. I'm fine. Terri's fine. You're fine. There's nothing for you to worry about."

Acute emotional sensitivity had grown along with Consuela's illness, and she started to softly cry at her daughter's passive-aggressive answer. Immediately Mona felt a twinge of guilt. She sat down on the sagging mattress and reached out to stroke her mother's feverish brow.

"I'm sorry, Mama."

By way of acknowledgment, Consuela tried to burrow her face into the network of lace bordering the sweat-stained pillowcase. Mona pulled back a braided, black hank of her mother's hair. She wanted to get a better look at the clotted patch of lavender welling up beneath the thin dry parchment of Consuela's skin. It trailed from the bottom of her right ear to just below the temple.

Mona sighed. "Mama, how many times have I told you to wake me up if you have to go to the bathroom in the middle of the night? You do that, you won't trip and fall in the dark and get these rainbow colors all over your face."

"You know I hate to wake you, especially how much trouble you have all the darn time just getting to sleep. Especially you gotta get up and go to the school every darn morning."

Mona shook her head in frustration.

"Besides, Terri told me she gonna have Merle come in here and gimme a good talking-to the next time I come in your room in the middle of the night. She say she gets woken up, too."

"What? She said she'd have Merle what?" Mona was out the door before Consuela could answer.

She slammed open the door at the end of the hall and stormed into the room she shared with her year older half-sister, Terri. Terri's snoring abruptly stopped as the doorknob hit her bedstead. Her badly-tinted carroty moptop stuck out in all directions from having been slept on. Then again, that was the way it was supposed to look 24-7. Fashion as auxiliary to laziness, Terri's outlook on life in general.

"Fuck, Mona!" Terri scooped up the alarm clock from the night table separating their twin beds, then heaved it across the room for emphasis. It clanged against the wall. "It's only seven-o'-fucking-clock in the goddamn fucking morning! Not all of us have to teach a bunch of lil' snotnose brats!"

Before Mona could respond, she saw something that made her blood hiss past the boiling point. Terri's beat-up set of works and a bent spoon lay atop a stack of paperbacks just inside the door next to her electric guitar. So, she'd been up herself since Mona had left the room. At least long enough to fix herself her wake-up then nod back off to dreamland. Mona kicked the rig and paperbacks across the clothes-strewn floor.

"Goddamn, Mona, I gotta get up an' kick yer sorry ass al –"

Before Terri could finish, Mona had her by the throat with both hands, pinning her against the wall.

"Shut the fuck up. Goddamn you, Terri. I can't believe my eyes. I know it's no use trying to make you stop until you're good and ready. But I've told you time and again to not be doing this shit when I'm around. You want to kill yourself, fine. I just don't want to see it. And I don't want Mama to see it, either."

Terri was going from beet-red to a darkening purple. Mona let up a bit, and Terri coughed out a big glob of phlegm on cue.

"Mama never comes in here. You know that. Stop the self-righteous shit."

"What's this about you telling Mama you're going to have Merle talking to her if she wakes us up to take her to the toilet?"

Terri twisted and knocked half-heartedly against Mona's iron grip. Mona let her go. Automatically, Terri massaged her neck, milking as much melodrama out of the situation as possible. She evaded the question.

"Fuck. You hurt me."

"Bullshit. Quit your whining. Now tell me about Mama and Merle."

"Nothing!"

"What do you mean, nothing?"

"Don't you have to be at work?"

Mona glanced at her wristwatch. "Yeah, but I'm not leaving this house till you tell me you'll never threaten Mama again.

Especially with Merle. She's scared to death of him."

"Merle's harmless." Terri let herself sink back down into her torn pillow.

"Yeah, right, Terri. That's why he's been in San Quentin twice."

"Merle'd never touch a hair on Mama's head. I wouldn't let him."

Mona snorted with derision. "You should have your own talk show. You are so full of shit."

"Fuck you." Terri pulled the sheet up around her neck.

Mona straightened her clothes as she stood up. "Terri, there's a big mess on the bathroom floor. If you only do one thing today, clean it up, okay? Before Mama has to go? Most of it's your crap anyway."

"I'd occasionally like to hear the word 'please' around here."

Mona looked away, knowing Terri was intentionally trying to keep the drama going so she would be late. "Please."

"Sure, Mon', anything you say."

Mona walked out of the room and down the hall.

Terri rubbed her eyes in aggravation.

"She sure knows how to ruin a girl's high."

# 3

Mona set down her briefcase as she started to leave the house. The side door to the kitchen was giving her trouble as usual, and she needed both hands to close it totally flush with the warped doorjamb and slight hump in the floor. Movement reflected in the door's dirty window caught her eye, and she smiled in spite of her foul mood.

Next door neighbor, Rose Martin, was hanging up her laundry in the adjoining yard. Her year old daughter kept her company, grabbing at the pink fuzz of her slippers. She would lunge her tiny body after the elusive furry feet every few inches her mother moved down the clothes line.

Unconsciously, Mona started to compare her looks to Rose. Rose was beautiful. What had Terri called her one time? Breathtakingly beautiful. Black hair in long tangled waves framing a delicate oval face. Green eyes glittering beneath heavy black brows that would have made any other girl look too masculine. But not Rose. It added to her special quality.

Mona stopped as she opened the door to her battered '71 Cutlass. Rose was deaf mute. She hadn't seen Mona yet, so Mona wasn't particularly self-conscious about staring. But what Mona wasn't sure of was Rose's bearings on where the baby was.

The little girl was laughing loudly at her failing attempts to get a hold of her mother's fuzzy slippers, and it seemed, judging by the way Rose moved, that she was unaware of her child underfoot. Just then Phil, Rose's husband came out their back door. He swang a lunchpail in one hand and a hardhat in the other, and Mona was distracted for a split second as she often was by Phil, his boyish good looks and graceful walk despite his good ole' boy carriage.

Rose caught sight of him out of the corner of her eye. Silently laughing, she whirled to meet him, sidestepping the baby without the slightest downward glance. Mona felt foolish. She didn't give Rose half as much credit as she deserved.

Phil spoke slowly and distinctly so Rose could read his lips. "I don't know, baby, I can't say for sure when I'll get home. You know this damn problem with the elections."

When she gave him a funny look, he put on his hardhat and set down his lunchpail. He started to sign as he spoke.

"The union elections, honey. You know I'm the only one with any concrete evidence that the thing was rigged. So they're definitely going to want me to stay. There's talk the DA might be coming by around five."

Rose suddenly leapt towards him, encircling his neck with her arms.

"Rose, Rose – " He pried her loose and moved his lips in exaggerated fashion inches from her face. "Now don't worry. I'm not going to let anyone hurt me. It's way too hot for them to pull anything right now."

Mona could tell Rose wasn't convinced. Phil was a bad liar. She didn't even know him that well and could tell.

"Hey, look who's here." He was waving at her now as he turned Rose around and, in one continuous motion, picked up the baby.

"Hi." Mona waved, signing "hello" for Rose's benefit.

Phil handed the little girl to Rose. She'd started to cry at being deprived of the pink slippers fuzzy company.

"Hey, when we gonna have that barbecue, Mona?" Phil kissed Rose on the cheek, then the baby as he shoved off towards the family station wagon parked next to the Cutlass.

Mona shrugged, frowning good-naturedly. "As soon as Terri gets off her ass and cleans it. It's filthy right now."

Phil started the car, popped it into reverse, then poked his head from the window as he eased out of the muddy dirt driveway onto the paved street. "No goddamn excuse. Tell her I'll do it. How about this weekend?"

Mona shrugged. "As long as I don't have to do any of the work. Terri gets too much of a free ride around here as it is."

Phil nodded and laughed as he pulled away.

Mona turned back to Rose. "You need anything at the store, for tonight? I can stop on the way home."

Rose smiled and shook her head.

"Okay, bye." Mona waved as she sunk into the ripped, once plush upholstery.

Rose waved, then took hold of the baby's hand and waved it gently back and forth, too. Both of them watched Mona accelerate down the street and disappear around the corner.

Almost immediately another car appeared from the opposite direction. It was a puke-brown Toyota slowly inching along the rutted pavement. It tentatively rolled to a stop at the lip of the Anderson/ Martin mutual driveway, then, after pausing for a few seconds, pulled in, not stopping until it rested on the grass beneath the clothesline right beside Rose.

Suddenly afraid, Rose took a few steps backward. She put one hand protectively over the baby's face.

The figure inside moved over to the passenger seat but clumsily goosed himself with the gearshift midway. He burst into a fit of cursing as he got himself settled, then leaned out the window to leer at Rose. She recognized the leathery, sunburnt face. It was Fred Lassiter, Phil's boss.

"Hey, you. Deaf and dumb girl. Where's your goddamn husband?" His voice was vicious and, even though it was only half past seven, already slurred with drink. Rose could smell it from where she stood. She was having a hard time understanding the specifics because of his slurring, but she picked up on his nasty demeanor.

"You dumb cunt, you can't hear a word I'm saying. D and D. Can't use your ears, can't use your tongue. I bet that pretty mouth is good for something. It's the only goddamn thing you're good for."

"You pot-bellied pig," Rose thought to herself. The baby began crying from Fred's bellowing, and Rose was doing her best to restrain herself from spitting in his face. Better not, she thought. He'd be the kind to wail on a defenseless woman and child.

"Well, I sure do hope your valiant hubby's gonna be D and D. He thinks he's being loyal to his union buddies, he's full of shit. He better not spill what he knows."

He hoisted himself partways out of the car window, his enormous gut undulating obscenely against the door. He gestured at her by flipping her off, then using his third finger for emphasis jabbing the air as he repeated his threat. "He – better – not – spill – what – he – knows – about – the – elections."

Tears ran down Rose's pale face. The baby clawed out at her, but Rose was totally oblivious.

As Lassiter awkwardly maneuvered himself back into the driver's seat, Rose saw her chance. She leaned over slightly into the Toyota passenger window and heaved a huge gob of spit onto Lassiter's meager bit of hair. By the time he'd straightened up, she was back exactly where she'd been standing, the baby still clutched to her breast. Lassiter snorted derisively, rammed the car into reverse, and came out so fast, Rose had to step back to keep him from hitting her. As it was, his bumper snagged one end of the clothesline pole and yanked it completely from the ground as he caromed into the street.

Terri had been awakened by all the shouting. She stood at her open bedroom window, looking at Rose as she put down the baby and tried to pull the clothesline back up into the yard.

"Jesus Christ. Can't nobody leave that poor girl alone?"

Terri slammed the window, stumbled a couple of steps and plopped down face first on her disheveled twin bed.

**4**

Rose sat on the lawn, hugging her knees. The baby crawled over, pulling herself vertical, and Rose wiped away her tears and picked up the child.

There was a screech of burning rubber, then the sound of spraying gravel which Rose couldn't hear. Merle's truck lurched to a halt where Mona's car had been parked in the muddy drive. Merle barely glanced at Rose as he jumped out, making a beeline to Terri's bedroom window. He opened it without hesitation and crawled through.

Terri was already snoring again in blissful, junked-out slumber. Merle exaggeratedly tiptoed to the side of her bed, smirking, surveying the syringe and blackened spoon on the cluttered night stand. He slid in beside her fully clothed. Terri fitfully surfaced from a deep sea.

"What the fuck do you want?"

Merle didn't like her grouchy tone, "What do you think?"

Terri was fed up and slapped at Merle, "Get out!"

He put his grimy hands beneath the covers and roughly fondled her. She softened, trying not to laugh.

"Stop it, Merle."

"Now you don't mean that, honey."

Annoyed, she nevertheless groaned with pleasure and turned over into his arms.

"You do know my weak points, don't you?"

He viciously pinched the hard, calloused nipples of her small, boyish tits. "More like your strong points."

Terri sighed. "Merle, you are the light of my pathetic life."

She stuck her tongue into his foul-smelling mouth.

She jumped, startled.

"What-the-hell is that!"

He tugged the sawed-off shotgun from beneath the sheet and tossed it clanking to the floor.

John Cullen, a plainclothes sheriff's detective just turned 40, stared out into the convenience store parking lot that was now blocked off and full of department vehicles. He noticed the lines in his face in the faint reflection from the slightly fogged window. The badge hanging around his neck looked decidedly dull and lusterless in the grey, overcast light from outside. Behind him the lab boys were surveying the carnage of the robbery massacre, sifting through the wreckage for forensic evidence. His uniformed superior, Sheriff Billie Travers, a tall, handsome woman in her late fifties, straightened up from the floor, the bloody pickaxe in a plastic-gloved hand. She was exasperated.

"What-the-hell you looking at, John? You've been staring out that window for the last ten minutes."

Cullen put his hands in his pockets and searched absent-mindedly for cigarettes. He was out. "There's some almost invisible blood spatter over here on the glass, guys. Looks almost like a dried red mist."

One of the lab techs looked up for a few seconds, jotted something down on a small pad of paper, then returned to help his colleague with the task at hand.

Travers frowned. "The boys have been here for hours and still haven't picked up much of anything we can use. There's prints on this," she held up the pickaxe, "but too smudged to do any good. The surveillance tape is toast, too. We're dealing with a real case here, John, I hope you realize. This boy, whoever he is, isn't going to stop here."

"You think he's local?"

"I wouldn't think so. I pray to God he isn't. I pray he moves on and causes some other county grief. Because unless we get damn lucky, we're not going to catch him right away. He's crazy, but he's smart, too."

"He doesn't look smart to me. He looks lucky."

Cullen puttered between the short aisles of convenience store crap, looking around with his hands still in his pockets. He plucked up a pack of Pall Malls from the cigarette display, then strolled into the rear of the store and outside through the back exit. Travers handed the pickaxe to one of the techs and followed.

The dirt parking lot behind U-Totem smelled like rotten vegetables, but Cullen knew that the store didn't sell vegetables, fresh or otherwise. He pondered the origin of the stench as he lit up an unfiltered cigarette, idly concluding that generic garbage must produce a certain consistent, malodorous bacteria, no matter what made it up.

Travers pulled off her plastic gloves and tossed them in a nearby rusty metal dumpster. There was a strange unspoken tension between her and Cullen.

"You feel like maybe having supper later?"

He wouldn't look at her. "I told you, Billie. It's over. I want to still be able to work with you, but otherwise – "

"John, who's to say there's anything wrong with two co-workers sharing a meal?"

Cullen blew out a puff of smoke, cocked his head to glance at her, then stared down at the ground. He let the cigarette fall and stubbed it out with one black boot. Shaking his head, he began to walk back into the store. Travers grabbed hold of his arm as he passed.

She was ticked off and on the defensive. "It's what happened with that union organizer guy down from Fresno last week – what's'is name? – Sanchez. That's it, isn't it? I'm not going to tolerate your superior –"

"I still can't believe that you'd do something like that, planting drugs in his car."

In front of anyone else, Travers could not have cared less, but with her ex-lover, she felt as if she had to justify herself. She knew she was on indefensible ground. "I told you the charges will get dropped when it comes up in court. Then he'll crawl out of town quietly with his tail between his legs."

Cullen pointedly detached her clutching hand from his upper arm. "What would your dad have said?"

Travers exploded with indignance. "He's been in the ground fifteen years, John. Give it a rest. I'm the sheriff now, not him. This is a different time and a different place from even ten years ago. This is the real world. You're not still at Berkeley."

Cullen was disgusted and could no longer look at her. He turned his back. "Billie, you know last week just brought everything to a head. It's been a long time coming…"

One of the lab boys stuck his head out the back door. "Sheriff, I got Jerry on the line."

Travers impatiently snapped at him. "Fine. I'll be right there."

Cullen seized the opportunity to walk past the technician and into the store.

Travers stood there alone, feeling as if she had a gaping hole in her chest, and she gazed vacantly at the dumpster.

Mona finished collecting test papers from her restless fifth grade. One particularly obnoxious boy with dirty blonde hair and a smudged, squashed-in-looking face, razzed his closest classmate. Mona swooped down on him.

"Tommy, I don't want to have to tell you again to stop that. You don't, you're going to find yourself on detention."

She turned her back, and he delivered a razz at her. She froze up, trying to control her temper, started to turn to reprimand him, but the bell rang. She shrugged her shoulders, giving up and motioned for the kids to leave. They screamed happily and rushed out. One little dark haired girl remained. Mona sat down at her desk and started to organize her papers. The little girl approached.

"Miss Anderson, I just want to tell you…I think you're a good teacher."

Mona smiled in spite of herself. "Thanks, Macy, honey. That means alot to me. I'll see you tomorrow, okay?"

The little girl nodded and toddled off. Mona wearily crammed her papers and a couple of books into her briefcase.

Another teacher, Millie Shaw poked her head in the open door. "I bet you're happy."

Mona was still distracted by the residual roar of fifth grade white noise that she'd been subjected to all day.

"What?"

"That it's two o'clock!"

Mona made a face and laughed. "I'm just so sick of the routine. I wish I was more farsighted so I could see the reward, how my influence and 'teaching – " she gestured, making quotation marks with her fingers, "– skills' will make a difference in their lives." Millie entered and jauntily sat down on one of the tiny desks. "You gotta use your imagination, girl. And you better have a good one. Better yet, stay out of the result, elsewise it'll drive you crazy." She paused, studying the worry lines in Mona's brow.

"How's Terri doin'? Is she really off the drugs?"

Mona shrugged again. "She says she is, but she isn't. I'd like to give her the benefit of the doubt. I don't see how I can. She lies to me all the time." Mona's voice almost started to slur with exhaustion. "Well, I'm going home."

"How about a drink."

Mona paused for a few seconds before answering, then smiled.

"Yeah, okay. I could use one."

**5**

Terri sat up on the edge of the rumpled bed and lit a cigarette. Merle, even after fucking Terri's brains out, was a bundle of nervous energy. He swung his legs over her head, grabbed his jeans from the floor and stood up into them, slipping them up along his taut, lizard-like limbs. A framed photo on the table between Mona's and Terri's beds caught his eye. He grabbed the picture of a beautiful Mexican woman who looked around thirty.

"Who the fuck is this?"

Terri blew out a smoke ring. "Mona's other half sister."

"You are shittin' me."

Terri shook her head of teased, spiky red hair and took the photo from Merle, studying it.

"She's a kid Consuela had with some Mex guy before she moved to Santa Mira and met Daddy." She set the picture back on the cluttered tabletop. "Her name's Manuela. Never met her though. She's in prison down there for murder. She's got to be around 45 now."

"Un-fucking-believable. Where's 'down there'?"

"Mexico City, I think."

Merle laughed to himself as he shuffled into the hall.

Terri sank down into her pillow and turned her head slightly to watch Merle, making sure he wasn't going to harass Consuela. But he headed past her bedroom door and made a right turn into the kitchen. Terri heard the refrigerator open and close, then the snap of a can opening. Merle reappeared, his head tilted, a beer glued upside down to his mouth as he dodged into the bathroom.

Merle pulled the door shut behind him and immediately stepped in the mess from Mona's morning tantrum. Since he was barefoot, he sensed it against his coarsened skin before he saw it. Right away something warm, red and sticky spread out beneath his right heel. He'd cut his arch on a piece of broken mirror and had barely felt it. Reaching over, he reeled off a wad of toilet tissue and, not thinking, clamped it against his gouged flesh. With his other hand he put down the already half empty can of Pabst on the generously clear expanse of the counter. He hopped one step backwards and propped himself against the towel rack.

He laughed at his reflection in the remains of the mirror, tracing his free hand along the two-foot scar running diagonally from the tip of his right shoulder to the bottom of his left rib. It furrowed nearly a quarter inch deep and tingled as he drew his finger-tips through it. Every time he did that he could not only feel but see his father straddling him, pinning him to the ground by kneeling on his twelve-year-old arms, scraping the red hot poker slowly, agonizingly across his scrawny frame. At the time, he'd tried to close his eyes against the look on the old man's face. But the soul-destroying madness flooding from his father's fiery eyes had made that impossible. His father's expression of obsessive hate and cruelty had transformed him, hypnotized him as a snake mesmerizes a bird, had nearly blotted out the incredible pain so the only thing he'd been able to feel was the warm sticky flow of his own blood soaking his entire chest and belly.

The bare chest and arms reflected back at him from the bathroom mirror weren't scrawny anymore. His forty-year-old frame was a massive labyrinth of coiled, iron-hard muscles, ropy sinews throwing even the tiniest capillaries into awesome relief. He looked away from the mirror to the crook of his right arm. Black pinpricks of scar tissue were emblazoned in the ghostly white, leathery flesh where he'd mainlined over and over. It was about time for a shot.

That made him think of things the asylum shrinks had said. Actually, one shrink in particular, the good-looking Dr. Marsha Grant. The good-looking, snobbish, head-up-her-ass and decidedly late

Dr. Marsha Grant. The feeling of his cock ramming into her suddenly chafed him as if it was happening all over again. Pulling at the crotch of his jeans, her words echoed in his throbbing head, "You know you're not doing this for the sex! It's all your low self-esteem!" Low self-esteem, low self-esteem, *low self-esteem!* That was after he'd ripped away her dress, but before he'd pushed his way inside of her. He winced at the thought of bringing the heavy glass paperweight down on her forehead to shut her up.

*"A sociopath with violent tendencies from a lower-class, low-income background. Bi-polar manic depressive. Possible paranoid schizophre8nic condition from puberty enhanced dramatically after murdering his father at the age of fourteen. Patricide has caused various delusions, including blaming his mother for the murder –"*

He slammed his palm against his forehead, trying to drive out the words. He wasn't even sure if he was remembering it right. He knew he was leaving some things out, some words he hadn't understood. The only reason he'd remembered "sociopath" and "patricide" was because he'd grabbed his file as an afterthought on his way out the window. He'd looked them up when he got to Darrell's house. Yeah, how could he ever forget those hundred dollars words? They were burned into his brain. He hated the word, "sociopath." Why not just call him a "psycho" and be done with it? That's the way he thought about himself. He didn't give a shit about anyone except himself, and sometimes he wondered if he even cared that much. "Psycho!" He enjoyed killing more than sex and dope. It was the one thing that made him feel really alive.

Grabbing the beer, he took a swig, looked up at the ceiling, gargled, then swallowed. Sweeping the debris on the floor aside with his still bleeding foot, he reached for the door and swaggered out into the hall. He paused outside Consuela's bedroom. A sadistic grin creased his face as he pressed it into the crack of the slightly ajar door.

"Merle, you asshole."

He jumped as if somebody had shoved their finger up his ass.

Terri was standing naked, hands on her hips, at the other end of the hall. She sashayed back into the bedroom.

"What!" He covered the distance in three exaggerated steps.

Terri was sitting on the edge of the unmade bed, her feet nervously snaking their way into the tangled sheet that drooped to the floor. "You're gonna wake her, that's what."

Not even glancing at Merle, she pulled the belt snug around her upper left arm. She registered immediately and let the plunger on the rig go. As the dope flowed into her veins, she tapped it the last centimeter home, smiled, tugged the fit free and licked away the spot of blood that abruptly materialized.

Merle didn't like the perturbed tone in her voice and matched it. "Why don't you pull the chair out from under the old bitch? And you and me can go on a cross-country tour. She's not even your own mother for Christ's sake! Your mother was white."

Terri's voice suddenly had a dreamy lilt to it that made Merle see red. "She's been more like a mother to me than my own, you stupid fucker! Just 'cause yer mama was a whore and yer daddy –"

He backhanded her so hard she banged her head against the greasy wall. "Terri, you don't shut your trap, I know someone who'll do it for you! Permanentlike!"

Unbelievably, Terri still felt like taunting him. "And who's that?'

"ME!"

She laughed.

Trembling, he walked away from her. It took every ounce of self-control not to grab her by the throat and throttle her.

**6**

The whole next day, Phil Martin couldn't get it off his
mind no matter how hard he tried. He'd forget it for a few minutes
while doing some particularly strenuous piece of work there in the
warehouse. But as soon as things let up, even for an instant, Lassiter's
sweaty, bloated face would intrude again, mouthing its obscene,
rasping excuse for a voice. Each and every time it'd take a couple of
seconds for Phil to translate the garrulous sounds into words, even
though the insults to Rose were lodged in his memory, like acid
poured on stone. The bastard. But he had to stop thinking about it,
had to keep from making this into a personal vendetta. Lassiter was
making a desperate attempt at doing just that, pulling him into a
grudge fight that would color everything with private feelings and
cripple his ability to pull the union together. The DA hadn't done
much the night before. He'd tried to bring a stenographer with him
but the one lone woman they had on payroll was still out sick with the
flu. They had mutually decided to reschedule for the coming Friday.

He wiped what seemed to be a river of sweat from his broad
forehead, glanced at his watch to see he still had two hours left to
quitting time, then rubbed the back of his hand against his already
drenched jeans.

Out of the corner of his eye he caught some furtive movement by the door to Lassiter's office. He turned his head from Harry Glass and the stalled forklift they were trying to push out of the way.

Lassiter was standing there across the warehouse, facing him and talking to two other men in suits who had their backs turned. Even though he couldn't see their faces, he could tell he hadn't seen them before. For a minute he made eye contact with Lassiter, and there was something in his expression that chilled him to the bone. He felt goosepimples rise along his forearm and shivered involuntarily at the nape of his neck.

All at once there was a whooshing roar from above.

Harry shouted at him, "Phil, look out!"

He glanced up by reflex. The dynamo crashing down blotted out his vision. He never knew what hit him.

## 7

The first thing Terri saw when she opened her eyes was the set of works lying on the floor beside the bed.

"Terri!" It was Consuela's voice coming from her room. Her door was shut and, although her voice was muffled, it cut through Terri like a knife, and she realized it was what woke her up.

"Terri!"

She scooted herself into a sitting position against the wall and, all at once, felt the knot that had grown on the back of her head as result of Merle's fit of temper. Rubbing it with one finger, she squinted against the light of the sinking late afternoon sun streaming in through the closed window. Merle had left and shut it after him – it had been open earlier before she'd nodded off. There was a muddy footprint on the sill heading out.

"Terri!"

She eased herself out of the bed, slowly planted her feet on the ground. "I'm coming, Mama! Goddamn it. Hold your goddamn horses."

Suddenly blood rushed and roared through her ears, and she steadied herself with one hand on the rickety bedstead to keep from falling over. The whooshing passed as quickly as it had come.

There was a beer can standing on the floor a couple of feet from Consuela's door. Fucking Merle.

When she opened the door a fetid, stale sickroom odor wafted over her. "It stinks in here, Mama. Why don't you open the window?"

"I'll catch cold, Terri." Consuela drew her lavender satin robe around her neck.

"What're you talkin' about? It's as hot as Satan's shithouse in here."

Consuela's tone went from one of self-pity to self-righteousness. "I've told you time and again, Teresa, I don't appreciate your gutter talk. I won't have it in this house."

Resigned to Consuela's obstinate ways. Terri shook her head and stumbled towards the window.

"Teresa, I told you I'd catch cold if we have that window open. Besides, they're making so much racket next door. I'll never get any rest."

Terri ignored her and, straining at the stubborn window, realized that there were noises coming from the Martin house. Abruptly, the window shot up. A breaking sound filled the room.

"What did I tell you? Rose is probably asleep and the baby's gotten at some dishes. With Rose being deaf, it could go on for hours."

Terri couldn't see much from where she was standing. The clothesline was filled with gently swaying white sheets obscuring view of the back kitchen door. Then, in between the short bursts of shattering, there was the constant low growl of a car coming up the street. Terri rubbed at her bleary eyes.

"Sounds like Mona…"

As usual Terri didn't pay any more attention to Consuela than she absolutely had to and kept her attention focused on the yard between the two houses. Sure enough, Mona pulled her Cutlass into the drive. It sank a bit on the right as a front tire grooved into the muddy rut Merle's pickup must have made when he had left.

As Mona climbed out, it struck Terri she looked as if she had the weight of the world on her shoulders. Poor Mona, the only responsible member of the family now that Papa Pete had kicked the tubercular bucket. Mona turning towards the Martin place reminded Terri a battle was raging a mere twenty yards away.

A shock of violent, uncontrollable fear jolted Terri back from the window. A black-and-white had pulled up on the other side of the clothesline. It wasn't until John Cullen, now in uniform, jumped out and made a beeline for the Martin's back door that Terri realized she wasn't about to get busted.

Mona shut her car door. She started for the Martin's, looked back over her shoulder as an afterthought and paused when she caught Terri at Consuela's window. A puzzled look creased Mona's pretty features. Terri shrugged in answer to the unspoken question. Mona stared down at the ground for a couple of seconds, then continued across the lawn.

A tall gangly woman with pale thin lips, glasses with coke bottle lenses and hair almost as black as Rose Martin's stood in the doorway with Rose's baby cradled in her arms. Her gaze was aimed at whatever was going on inside the kitchen. Miraculously, the baby wasn't crying at the ongoing din of breaking crockery. Mona paused as the woman turned towards her with a dumb stare.

"What's the matter? Is Rose – ?"

The woman seemed incapable of speech. Her mouth hung slightly open in an expression of awestruck disbelief. Mona recognized the soothing, yet urgent tone of a man's voice coming from the dim recesses of the kitchen. She beheld a vision of wanton, desperate destruction as she rounded the corner past the woman and infant. Cullen held a struggling Rose by both her shoulders on a carpet of disintegrated glass and porcelain. Rose had her head bowed, refusing to look the deputy in the eye, all the time uttering inarticulate gasps and the kind of mewling noises a cat might make if capable of the emotion of despairing frustration. Suddenly she became limp and let the dish – what looked to Mona to be the last intact piece of china in the room – fall. It cracked into three large pieces as it hit the floor.

"What's wrong?" Mona realized as soon as she opened her mouth that her voice was much angrier than she'd meant it to be. Cullen jerked his head around as if struck from behind but didn't let his grip on Rose relax.

"She's deaf and dumb," admonished Mona, "in case you hadn't realized that yet."

Cullen's face went a deep crimson. "No, I didn't realize it. She was already like this when I got here, and I thought it was the shock of the news."

"What news?"

"Who are you? A relative?'

Rose had sunk into a staring-into-space inactivity since she'd sensed Mona's presence, and Cullen looked back down at her.

"I'm Mona Anderson. I live next door. Why in God's name would she be – ?" Then it struck her, and she felt she was going to be sick. "It's Phil, isn't it?"

He nodded while keeping his eyes on Rose. "He was killed in an accident at the plant this afternoon. A big motor or dynamo or something fell on him." Rose had been watching his lips and, all of a sudden, burst into renewed frenzy.

Cullen tried to look at Mona while holding onto Rose. "Are you close to her at all? You want to give this a shot, try to calm her down?"

Mona only hesitated for a second, then walked decisively across the room. Firmly but gently she took hold of Cullen's right arm, and, without taking her eyes off of Rose, moved him aside. He grimaced, shook his head, then relaxed. He folded his arms and leaned against the counter beside Rose, all the time watching Mona's actions.

Rose's eyes were darting back and forth between Mona and Cullen, and an unstoppable flood of tears flowed from them, covering her beautiful pale porcelain complexion with a gleaming film. The wetness made her seem to glow from within in the faint light of dusk that permeated the kitchen.

Mona took her head in both hands, forcing Rose to look only at her. She spoke in carefully enunciated words, slowly and deliberately letting her mouth work so that Rose could easily read her lips.

"Rose, honey, I'm here. I'll help you. Stop now. Stop all this craziness. Okay?"

For nearly a minute Rose just continued to stare into Mona's face. Then, slowly she nodded.

"Everything okay?" Mona and Cullen both turned around at the sound of Terri's voice.

"No, Terri, nothing's okay. Phil got killed at the plant."

A strange look came over Terri's face, shocked back to reality from her high.

Rose crumpled to her knees. Mona kept her eyes on Cullen as she sank down to the floor beside her.

"It's okay. She's…she'll be all right now. You can go, officer – "

"Officer Cullen. Actually Detective John Cullen. I just got promoted. I'm usually not in uniform anymore. Habits die hard." He sighed after introducing himself, and Mona looked back at Rose. He shook his head sadly, then pushed himself off from the counter and made for the back door.

Terri stepped in front of him, blocking his way.

"What happened to Phil?"

He stared at Terri as if seeing her for the first time. He'd completely forgotten anyone else was in the room. Mona was affecting him strangely. He realized finally that she was what was causing his disorientation. He'd been on the force plenty long enough to be hardened against telling wives and husbands about the deaths of their mates, so Rose's muted hysteria wasn't what was getting to him. Something about Mona and the way she had looked at him had struck him to the core, burrowed beneath his tough layer of hard-heartedness.

He tried to push past Terri. He could she was coming on way too aggressively and was undoubtedly trying to pick a fight, get a rise out of him. She latched onto his arm. He stopped dead in his tracks and let his eyes stab into her face. His stare was so intense, Terri averted her gaze. Yet she didn't let him go. He plucked at her fingers, prying them from around his elbow.

"They don't know exactly. Not yet anyway. He was standing on the floor of the warehouse when a dynamo they were trying to load into a hoist up above on the split level slipped and fell on him. It looks like it could have been just – "

" – an accident, hunh? Yeah, right." Terri's interruption made him blush again. Terri glared past him to Mona and Rose.

Partly trying to quiet his own misgivings, he continued. "I know there was trouble inside the union. Rumors have been running riot about the last election. But we don't have proof of anything yet. There's going to be an investi – "

"Oh, shit. Why don't you fuckin' cops do something for once! Hunh?"

The savagery of her anger took him by surprise and everything he had always hated about being a cop, all the radical clichés he himself had put stock in when he was in his early twenties in the sixties crowded in around him. It was as if they were tangible living things. He was speechless. When he saw the way Mona was staring at him, his heart started hammering in his chest. He turned away from them and, nearly knocking over the open-mouthed woman holding the baby, rushed out into the twilight.

"Terri, can't you ever shut your big mouth? He was okay."

Terri grimaced but didn't offer any more of her opinions.

"Do you think you could lower yourself to give me a hand with Rose?"

Embarrassed, Terri moved quickly to Rose's other side and helped Mona lift her to her feet.

"We'll take her over to our place. She can sleep in our room tonight."

Terri started to say something but immediately thought better of it and kept her mouth shut.

Mona paused as they led Rose out of the crockery-littered kitchen. The woman in the doorway with the baby was trembling.

"Are you related to Rose?"

The woman could barely talk and just nodded. Terri knew who she was and introduced Mona.

"This is Jessie." She looked at the woman. "You're Rose's sister, right?"

Jessie held the now-quiet baby's head close to her breast and mumbled, "Yeah..."

Mona put her free hand that wasn't draped around Rose's shoulders on Jessie's arm. "Can you take the baby for a couple of days?"

Jessie suddenly snapped out of it. She wiped her tears away with the back of her wrist. "Oh, yes. It won't be any trouble."

The sun was going down, and the dim light made the sparsely populated woodland across the road look malevolent and menacing. Mona and Terri steered Rose across the lawn to their house. Jessie, babe in arms remained petrified at the Martin's house kitchen door, watching them.

Cullen was still sitting in the black-and-white, quietly studying the scene. When he saw that Mona had the situation under control, he switched on the headlights, then backed out and slowly rolled off down the street.

Mona, both of her arms around Rose, nudged the back door with her hip and entered the kitchen. She immediately noticed something off and sniffed the air. "What's that?"

Terri, bringing up the rear on the other side of the mute woman, wrinkled her nose. "Smells like smoke."

They swiftly carted Rose down the hall and set her limp form down on the floor as they rushed into Consuela's room.

The lampshade on her bedside table was aflame, set on fire by the candle next to it. Mona swatted the lamp off the tabletop, and Terri smothered it with a throw rug.

"Jesus Christ."

Mona sat down on the edge of the bed and tried to rouse Consuela, but she was out cold.

"Mama! Mama!"

Terri stood watching in suspense while Mona revived Consuela by massaging her cheeks. Mona petulantly looked over her shoulder at her sister.

"Terri, open that window."

Terri was embarrassed she was slow on the uptake and rammed up the window frame so violently that the glass rattled. Suddenly, Consuela came awake and, with almost superhuman strength, bolted from Mona's arms and out of the room. Hysterical, she ricocheted against the door into the hall, then bounced into the wall where Rose stoically waited.

"He's trying to kill me. He don't want me around so I can keep him from Terri."

Rose was unaware of her surroundings and didn't even look up, but Consuela began a conversation with her anyway.

"Terri's man, Merle…he wants me dead. I know he does. I woke up when he set fire to the lampshade."

Mona and Terri cautiously approached her and grabbed her as they would have a frightened cat.

"Mama," Terri's voice was gently reproachful. "Hush." She put a comforting arm around her stepmother and led her back into the bedroom. Mona rearranged the bedclothes and pulled them down as Terri sat Consuela on the dank, fetid mattress.

Mona tucked her in as Terri smoothed back the old woman's hair.

"Mama, Merle doesn't want to kill you. He doesn't want to kill nobody."

Mona rolled her eyes, shook her head and left the room. Terri remained sitting on the edge of the bed, lulling Consuela to sleep.

In the hall, Mona helped Rose up and steered her down to her bedroom. She was appalled at the unsightly mess Terri had made of

the room during the day. Then, as she sat Rose down on her twin bed on the far side of the room, she noticed Merle's muddy footprints on the battered hardwood floor. She frowned, trying to figure out what they'd been up to – besides sex – when she'd been away at school. She gently helped Rose out of her dress and into a bathrobe, then pulled back the sheet and blanket and lay her down on the bed.
She began undressing herself as she walked back down the hall to Consuela's room. She was falling into a blacker mood by the second.

"Merle better not be coming over here tonight."

Terri lashed out. "He ain't comin'. He had to go down to San Bernardino on business and won't be back until day after tomorrow."

Mona turned to leave, then stopped as something occurred to her. She couldn't resist rubbing it in. "Merle doing 'business'? Isn't that a violation of his parole?"

Terri flipped her off.

Mona returned to the bedroom.

She crawled into bed facing Rose. The shivering woman was curled in a fetal position. Mona pulled up the sheet and blanket and put her arms around her. She made sure Rose was watching her as she spoke.

"Rose, try to relax. I'm here. I'm going to take care of you. Tomorrow-we'll-find- out-what-happened-to-Phil."

## 8

The dawn's early light seeped into the room. Terri slept with her pillow over her head. Mona had been tossing and turning all night and came fitfully awake when she realized that Rose was gone. She sat bolt upright.

"Terri, Terri."

Terri was dead to the world and didn't hear her.

"Terri!" Mona threw a pillow at her, and Terri finally peeked out from under her covers. She had a pissed-off expression on her face and grabbed the clock between their beds.

"What-the-fuck, Mona? It's six-thirty in the goddamn morning. I don't have to get up and go to work like you do."

"Where's Rose? Did you see Rose leave?"

It dawned on Terri that Mona's concern might be warranted, but she barely changed her belligerent attitude.

"I don't know. I didn't see her. I was sleeping. Hell, maybe she's in the bathroom."

Mona jumped from the bed, dashed out of the room but was back almost immediately.

"Fuck. She's not in the house."

She quickly climbed into jeans and a T-shirt. "I've got to be at work in an hour. I've got a bad feeling."

Terri punched her pillow several times, frustrated with her precious sleep being interrupted. "So? Rose is okay. If she left, she left 'cause she wanted to."

"I've got a bad feeling."

"You said that already. Leave me the fuck alone."

At Springer-Harris Tool and Die, Fred Lassiter was sitting, engrossed in his work, making notes on a checklist clamped onto a clipboard. His desk was set off from a large secretarial pool. There were two rows of six desks apiece, about half of them filled with middle-aged matrons and young women with teased bouffant hairdos.

Rose Martin materialized through a door at the far end of the large, oblong office and tentatively walked down the aisle between the rows towards Lassiter. She was frightened, yet simultaneously calm and purposeful. Nearing Lassiter, she reached into the folds of her dress and pulled out a revolver. Several secretaries nearest her stood up and backed away. Then one of them screamed. Surprised and disoriented, Lassiter's head jerked up. When he spotted Rose, a cold sweat broke out all over his corpulent body.

"What-the-hell you doin'?"

Rose came to a stop, standing stock still only a few feet away, the revolver pointed straight at Lassiter's heart. Her crystal blue eyes were like chips of ice. They filled with tears, beginning to melt.

"I didn't have nothin' to do with what happened to Phil. Honest." The tenor of Lassiter's voice was astonishingly different from the last time he'd spoken to Rose. But being deaf, she could not hear the dramatic change, only see it in his terrified stare.

"Girl, think what you're doing. You got a baby, right? What'll happen to your baby? This won't bring Phil back."

Several seconds passed, the only sounds Lassiter's labored breathing and the shuffling steps of retreating employees. Rose took a deep breath, then shot Lassiter three times in the chest. The stunned supervisor crumpled as blood erupted across his white, shortsleeve shirt.

The place emptied as Rose walked around the desk and put one last bullet in the fallen man's brain.

Mona burst into the Martin house kitchen, searching for Rose. The broken china still littered the yellow linoleum.

"Rose! Ro – Shit. She can't hear me."

The wall phone rang, and Mona grabbed the receiver before it had time to ring again.

"Yes?"

"Hello, is this Rose Martin's sister?" It sounded like the cop, Cullen.

"No, it's Mona Anderson from next door. Who's this?"

"John Cullen from the Sheriff's Department. Listen, Rose is down at the plant with a .38 revolver. She just killed Fred Lassiter. She's holed up in there, and Sheriff Travers is on the way."

"Oh my God."

"I called because I want to get someone over there who can talk to her, so to speak. Billie Travers will take a hard line with her, deaf mute or not."

"I'll meet you – "

"No, wait there. It's on my way. And I've got the siren and lights."

"I'll be outside."

Mona raced through the kitchen door and stopped at the edge of the road. Trembling, she pulled out a cigarette, lit it, but only took a couple of puffs before throwing it to the ground. She began pacing.

There were three patrol cars pulled up to the entrance of the factory offices. Billie Travers was the first out, then deputies Jerry Sebring, Tom Guiterrez and Marv Schamel. Several secretaries were nervously milling around, chain-smoking Kool menthols. Two high-powered executives, the tall, black-haired, phlegmatic Holly Harris and balding, obese Steve Springer glided over as one unit to meet the sheriff and her men.

She shook hands with them, a curious grin threatening to widen into a smile. "Well, gentlemen, it looks like we've got a situation here."

Harris could not contain his fear and anger. "It's more than just a 'situation,' it's a goddamn powderkeg!"

Soft-spoken and sensible Springer looked towards the deputies behind Travers, then gently took her by the arm and pulled her a yard or two out of their earshot. He let his words ooze out in a conciliatory but firm tone.

"Holly's right, Billie. We can't afford to have this get in the papers."

Travers gave them a condescending smile. "You mean the paper you don't hold an interest in."

"Listen, Travers, don't get holier-than-thou on us." Harris was ready to explode.

"Now calm down, Holly." Springer touched Harris' shoulder as he spoke, but his lanky partner yanked himself away. "Jeez, Holly, I mean it, take it easy. Billie knows the position we're all in with this. Everyone knows Phil Martin was getting his nose into places with his organizing. Places that were none of his goddamn business. Our workforce knows it."

Harris could not quell his anxiety. "Yeah? You think that that's good, you idiot? The press knows it, too. Out-of-town press. They could turn this whole thing into a three-ring circus. They're already saying that that Sanchez fuck from Fresno got framed on the drug charge."

Travers delighted in seeing them squirm. When she finally decided to speak, her tone was sardonic. "Now, Mr. Harris, there aren't going to be any circuses. Three-ring or otherwise. I've already taken care of the reporters – " she gestured behind her, " – and there's not going to be anybody from the press coming past those factory gates."

Springer tried to put a positive spin on things. "It's a good thing most of the pro-union workers aren't here today. Ninety percent of them went over to Martin's folks' house in Santa Mira."

Looking over Travers shoulder, Harris got pissed off again. "You spoke too soon."

Phil's best friend, Mel Dempsey, roaring drunk, shouldered his way through the deputies and onlookers. "What-the-fuck, you sons-a-bitches! I don't care how many cold-blooded dog-bastards Rose killed, you ain't gonna go in there and shoot her down."

Travers slowly turned, a bemused smirk on her face as she nodded her head at the deputies. It was nearly impossible with his massive, flailing frame, but they managed to somehow restrain the obstreperous Dempsey.

"Fuck you! Fuck all you murderers!"

They dragged him off towards the closest cruiser and started to slap on the handcuffs.

Travers stepped towards them. "That's okay. Let him go.

Just keep him outside the gate."

The uniformed men, respecting Dempsey's size, let the cuffs fall away, then gingerly pushed and shoved the big man towards the opening in the fence.

Travers raised her voice. "You better stay out there and settle down, Mel. Otherwise you know what happens."

Harris and Springer stared at her as if she was crazy. She ignored them and turned to face a short, stout secretary standing close by.

"All right, where is she?"

The woman took one last puff then ground her spent cigarette against her heel. "Right inside. She is definitely still there. We haven't heard a peep."

"Not surprising – since she can't talk."

The secretary frowned at the sarcasm, but Travers was already stalking purposefully into the building.

Harris and Springer turned back to each other once she had disappeared and continued their under-their-breath damage control. Harris' face was blotchy with a nerve-stoked red rash. "We should never have hired that loose cannon Chambers."

Springer finally lost his temper. "That is completely on you, Holly. I was crazy to go long with you. Hiring some strong-arm nutcase because he sells coke to your ex-wife. I wanted to take Brantwell's advice and bring in his man from L.A."

They stopped whispering as Deputy Jerry walked by, following Travers into the entranceway.

Rose sat listlessly on the edge of Lassiter's desk, staring at his empty chair. She held the gun carelessly, letting it hang at her side. As if having a fit, she suddenly shivered, swung open the revolver's chamber, then reloaded from a cache of bullets in the pocket of her housedress. She glanced around the empty secretarial pool. There was nothing. She turned back to Lassiter's chair. Her husband Phil Martin was there now, cuddling their baby, Lassiter's bloody corpse at his feet. Phil took the baby's tiny hand.

"C'mon, honey, wave at Mommy. C'mon now, wave at Mommy."

There was a loud bang from the opposite end of the room but, of course, Rose did not hear it. But feeling a low vibration in the floor, she slowly turned around. Fred's chair was once more empty behind her. At the opposite end of the space, Travers and Deputy Jerry were positioning themselves behind a desk just inside the double doors. Rose noticed the tufts of their hair and abruptly swung the gun up, squeezing off a shot.

Travers ducked into a deeper crouch and Jerry literally flattened himself spread- eagled on the dirty linoleum floor.

He looked up at his boss. "Anything I can do?

Travers was at a loss, something rare for her controlling persona. "I don't know what either of us can do besides shoot her. She can't hear a word we say."

Rose suddenly strode down the aisle between the desks. She held the .38 straight out in front of her, smiling.

"Fuck, here she comes!" Travers rose straight up to her entire six foot height and calmly shot Rose through the heart.

## 9

There were two fire department ambulances pulled up to the entrance of the factory office building. John Cullen's car screeched to a halt between them, and he and Mona piled out. Travers, Jerry and several other deputies were walking slowly out of the main office building. They were followed by two paramedics with Rose's corpse on a stretcher between them, then two more with Lassiter's body. There was an audible collective gasp from Mona and the secretaries as one of Rose's arms slipped from beneath the sheet to trail a slick of blood along the ground.

Mona was all but in a state of shock. Cullen put his arm around her shoulders, and Travers stopped short, watching the two.

Mel Dempsey sat on the curb about ten yards away, just inside the lot gate, his tearstained gaze dejectedly following Rose as she was loaded into the ambulance.

Mona lunged at Travers, but Cullen held onto her. "You murdering fucking bitch."

Travers frowned. "You think I wanted to? She came at us shooting. She couldn't hear anything we said." Despite her steel-edged resolve barely softening, she flinched under Mona's stare.

"Maybe she's better off now anyway."

Mona spat out her words. "You've no right to judge that."

She spotted the cowering executives who were trying to stay in the background behind Travers. Mona tore herself from Cullen's grip and stepped closer.

"And you, you bastards. I know the trouble Phil was getting himself into. And you're stupid if you don't think everyone here knows you had something to do with his death."

Harris and Springer turned away, but Travers held her ground, staring coldly at Mona. "Miss Anderson, we shouldn't say things we might end up regretting later."

"You think I'm going to let this rest here, you're crazy. There are newspapers and federal commissions who're going to want to know all about this."

Cullen forcibly wrested her backwards, yanking her towards his cruiser. He whispered in her ear as he dragged her along. "You're the one who's crazy, talking to cold-blooded cutthroats like that."

They climbed into the car while the small silent crowd next to the ambulances watched them. Cullen backed the vehicle slowly out of the lot.

Harris gave Travers a dirty look and whispered his own aside to Springer.

"Something's going to have to be done about the Anderson girl, too."

Two reporters from a Fresno TV station tried to flag them down, but Cullen shifted into drive and took off. Mona shook her head in disgust.

"I don't believe this. This cannot be happening." She tried to catch her breath. "Where are they taking her?"

"The morgue."

"Who's going to look after the baby? Her sister Jessie's already got five kids."

He shook his head and didn't answer. Mona stared at him for a few seconds, then straight ahead into empty space.

Things had quieted down, and Harris walked to where his car was parked at the far end of the lot. Merle was standing nearby against a stretch of chain link fence. Harris spoke furtively without looking at him.

"Nice work, psycho. I told you to lay off Martin till we gave you the word. Now you've gotten us all in a pretty mess.

"You and Springer are a couple of candy asses. How many times have you given me 'the word' on that cocksucker before this, then put the brakes on at the last minute? Fuckin' pussies. He needed takin' out. He was no better than a goddamn commie. I did the job – maybe a little sooner than you wanted, but there's no harm done."

"What planet are you living on?"

Merle chuckled. "Planet Motherfucker in the galaxy of Merle."

Harris shook his head. "A comedian, too. You and Shecky Greene."

Merle frowned at the sarcasm and tried to reassure him. "You worry too much. Nothing's going to happen."

"Let's hope not, asshole – for your sake."

Merle's suddenly red hot face said that this was clearly not the way to talk to him, but Harris' over-inflated ego and sense of entitlement kept him from noticing, and Merle, fighting a homicidal impulse, bit his tongue. Harris climbed into his El Dorado. "Now, because of your decided lack of subtlety, I may need you for another job. But we're going to have to wait a while. We pull anything else now, it's going to be too obvious."

"Who?"

"That troublemaker schoolteacher, Mona Anderson."

Merle smiled.

Just out of earshot, despairing and despondent Mel Dempsey sat on the curb about twenty feet away. He was in that sodden state of drunk-but-not-quite-drunk-enough-to- make-that-difference he so desperately wanted. He glanced up as Harris screeched out of the lot and then noticed Merle standing against the fence. Merle sneered at him, pushed himself away from the clanking metal links and walked to his pickup truck. Dempsey's brow knit. He felt vaguely troubled, yet couldn't put his finger on exactly why.

Cullen pulled the cruiser to the dirt curb in front of the Anderson house. Neither he nor Mona made a move to get out, both of them just sat staring straight ahead. He gently laid his right hand over her left. After a couple of seconds, Mona pulled her hand away.

# 10

Terri paced the living room in the late afternoon shadows. She picked up the phone on the first ring.

"What?" She paused. "What-the-hell do you mean, Merle? I wanted a couple of balloons, that's it…I don't want you bringing in a couple of ounces…Unh, hunh, yeah, right…so that's what you got the gun for. Yeah, sure, tell me more fairy tales…Don't you tell me you haven't been breaking and entering around here. I know you…no, you fucking shut up. I know why you were in the joint in the first place…"

Something Merle said seemed to sober her, and she sat down on the threadbare couch, chastened. "All right, okay, okay…I said okay, go ahead. Bring it over Sunday during the day then…I'll make sure Mona won't be here…yeah, okay…I said okay." She banged down the receiver.

Mona walked through the front door.

"What's the matter with you? Your school called."

Mona, her face pale and drawn, stared at Terri for a few seconds, in a daze. When she spoke, her voice was stoic. "Rose is dead."

The dirty pink house Merle pulled up in front of in Glen Cove was badly in need of a paint job, and the asphalt of the driveway was crumbling. He parked behind a dilapidated Cadillac, then walked briskly across the overgrown, weed-choked lawn. South American dance music was blaring from inside the living room. He banged on the front door.

Short, blonde Lucy, one of the three female dope dealers who lived there, opened the door a crack, then wider when she saw it was Merle. Bettina Jones, their defacto ringleader was gyrating in a sexy dance in the background. Bettina smiled at Merle but made no move to turn down the music and kept on dancing.

These chicks made him fidgety. "So, have you got the stuff ready?"

Lucy shrugged.

"What does that mean?"

Lucy gestured at Bettina. "Ask her."

The third girl, Cathy, shouted from the kitchen, "Are we going to finish making these goddamn cookies or not?"

Lucy shouted back, "Hold your horses. I'll be right there."

Bettina still refused to give up her dervish-like rapture. Cathy, a tall, tattooed drink of water with two-tone blonde/brown hair, strutted angrily into the living room, headed for the ghetto blaster.

"Can we stop listening to this goddamn fucking fag music?"

She took out the CD, flipped it at the perturbed Bettina, who deftly caught it as it sailed by. Cathy inserted another CD and abruptly a very loud female heavy metal band was blasting. She smiled. "That's more like it." Finally, she noticed their company. "Oh, hey Merle –" She returned to the kitchen.

Lucy looked at Bettina, then Merle, shook her head and followed Cathy out of sight.

Bettina was feeling resentful and muttered under her breath. "Fuckin' bitch."

"Hey, can we get this show on the road?"

Bettina gave him a flinty-eyed stare and plopped down on the couch. She reached under the sofa and pulled out a canvas bag and scale.

Merle's eyes lit up. "Great. We don't have to weigh it. I'm in a hurry. I know you guys wouldn't fuck me."

She fired up a cigarette and sank lazily back into the sofa cushions.

"You mean we wouldn't dare. Right?"

He sat down next to her.

They could hear Lucy and Cathy shouting in the kitchen. "We have to fold in the goddamn eggs."

"We don't put the eggs in yet. Are you out of your mother-fuckin' mind?"

Bettina and Merle continued to stare at each other.

"How much?"

"I told you already."

"I can't pay that. It's not that I don't have the bread. It's just that your price is a royal fuck job."

"That is just too goddamn bad, Merle. Take it or leave it."

Merle was quietly starting to boil. "I told you Bettina. I can't pay that."

Bettina's eyes looked down.

Merle's right hand whisked aside his suit jacket to expose the automatic tucked in his belt. He caressed the butt, and he gave her a smarmy smile.

"So don't pay it, Merle. Get on your trusty steed and scram."

He made a grab for the bag, but Bettina clutched at his hand. "No. Pay up or leave."

"I'm not paying that price."

"Why is that again, Merle?" It was Cathy's voice. He turned to find her in the kitchen doorway behind him, dipping the barrel of her Glock into the mixing bowl cradled in the crook of her left arm, then withdrawing it to lick batter off the barrel's sight. She smiled.

Merle sped along in his truck and banged his fist on the steering wheel, beside himself with anger. "Fuck!"

Terri sat by herself on the hood of Mona's car. The wind was blowing slightly, and some of the laundry that Rose had left out on her clothes-line was whipping about. A dress suddenly tore loose and flew to the ground a few yards away. Terri got off the car and stooped down to pick it up, reverently folding it and pressing it to her breast.

The heavy metal girl band was still roaring from the ghetto blaster in Bettina's living room. Bettina's voice rang out over the din, "I don't give a fuck. I'm turning this shit off." Suddenly it was quiet.

Bettina and Cathy stood with their hands on their hips,

fuming silently at each other. Lucy folded her arms.

There was a clanking sound from outside the front door. They stared at the battered wood, united in a paralyzing fear. Cathy came further into the room, setting the mixing bowl down on the couch and drawing her gun.

Bettina exclaimed, "Christ – !" then abruptly the door was knocked down. They were open-mouthed with shock. Cathy let off a round, and there was an immediate response from outside as she was whacked bloodily in the chest with buckshot and sent sprawling on the sofa, dead. Bettina and Lucy stared down at her corpse, then backed away from the door.

Billie Travers voice rang out from the darkness beyond. "You two –"

Travers, Jerry and another deputy materialized out of the darkness, guns drawn.

"Put your hands over your head."

## 11

John Cullen was depressed, driving aimlessly in his cruiser, when Travers' came over the radio.

"John, we got what you might call a lead on that convenience store murder."

He picked up the mike and acknowledged the call. "10-4, Billie. What about it?"

"Those heroin dealers over in Glen Cove. We busted them about an hour ago. Took one of them out. An early '60s Dodge pickup was spotted beside the house earlier, one similar to the one spotted at the convenience store. Anyway, we took some plaster molds of the tire tracks in the muddy driveway. They match the tracks from in front of the store."

Cullen pressed the talkback. "What do you want me to do?"

"Just keep on the lookout for now. He'll turn up."

"Right."

Annoyed, he clicked off the radio.

Cold dawn sunlight filtered through tree branches onto the frosty lawn of the Anderson house. Inside the living room, Mona sat on the edge of a beat-up easy chair, looking out the window.

Terri came in brushing her teeth.

"Terri, don't get mad, but I want to ask you something."

Terri removed the toothbrush from her mouth and glared at her with apprehension.

"What do you see in Merle?"

Terri shook her head, building up a head of steam.

"Terri, I'm really not trying to hurt you. I really want to know."

Terri became serious, quelling her temper. "As pathetic as it sounds, he's the only guy I've ever been with that I felt really needed me."

Mona frowned and stared back out the window. Terri shrugged, resumed brushing her teeth and stalked out of the room. The phone rang, and Mona answered it before Terry could make it back in.

"Hello?" Her voice grew cold and grudging, "Just a minute..." She covered the receiver with her hand and shouted "Guess who."

Terri smiled, yanked the phone away and whispered to her, "He's also great in bed."

Mona stood up to walk out. "*That* I don't believe."

Terri didn't hear her, transfixed by her man's domineering voice.

"Yeah?...Listen, Merle, I'm not going to be here. I got to go to a funeral today with Mona. Then I have to go straight over to that pisshole they call a club –"

Merle was slumped against the wall in the bar's mahogany paneled phonebooth, a drink in one hand and the receiver in the other. He was ticked off.

"You didn't tell me your band was playing tonight."

Mona got up and walked out of the room.

"Yeah, I did too tell you we were playing. Don't worry, the way things have been going it's probably our last gig."

Merle was still not happy, Terri could tell by his tone. "What about your mother?"

Terri lowered her voice. "She's here sleeping and you better not wake her...Yeah, just bring it over and do what you gotta do while we're gone. I'll leave the back door open...yeah, yeah –"

Stoic, staring-into-space Merle distractedly hung up the receiver and downed his shot.

It was a little after one in the afternoon, and Terri drove while Mona sat in the passenger seat of the stuttering Oldsmobile, staring out the window. There was some crappy, innocuous MOR rock playing on the radio.

"Mona, I know how you feel about Rose. I felt close to her, too. But look at it this way, what would she have done, how could she have gone on without Phil?"

"Fuck you, Terri. How can you say that? You, of all people. You're the strong fucking bitch who won't take shit from anybody and can live hand-to-mouth if you have to. Rose would have been fine. If she hadn't given Fred Lassiter what he deserved. She could've managed just fine. I would've helped her. Her sister and Phil's folks would've helped her."

"The point is darlin,' that ain't what happened. She blew her top. And who can blame her? In a goddamn silent world where she didn't feel at home, where she probably thought Fred and the rest of those corrupt sons-o'-bitches would never ever get theirs."

Mona had no answer for that.

"She went out in a big explosion, Mona. Just like she was askin' for it. She might as well've sent Billie Travers an engraved invite to plug her."

They pulled up a narrow dirt road at the top of the cemetery and stopped.

"I can't believe they got a double funeral together so quick. Phil and her both."

"Phil's folks wanted to get it over with." Mona sighed. "They're leaving town with the baby tomorrow. They're going back east."

"You go ahead. They don't want to see a good-for-nothing like me." Terri remained in the car while Mona got out. She strolled briskly down a slight incline, making her way amongst trees and gravestones.

Rose and Phil were being buried in a twin plot. Cullen stood on one side, a minister in the center and Phil's folks with Rose's sister Jessie on the other side. Mel Dempsey stood a few yards away, obviously nursing a hangover.

Sheriff Billie Travers had stationed herself at a distance, partially hidden by a giant monument. A large raven was perched on a nearby tombstone, occasionally breaking the drone of the preacher's platitudes with its cawing.

As Mona stopped next to Cullen, she looked over her shoulder and glared at Travers. They had gotten there late. The minister finished, and he and Phil's folks slowly turned to leave. They made no move towards Mona, and Mona, feeling awkward at not knowing them, did not feel comfortable taking the initiative. Jessie tried to smile at Mona as she joined Phil's folks but it quickly turned into tears and she had to look away.

Two cemetery workers immediately began filling in the graves.

Mona shook her head, disgusted. "It's hard to believe more of their friends aren't here. Phil was a pretty well-liked guy."

Cullen watched Phil's family trail off and didn't look at her. "They're afraid. Afraid for their measly jobs. Afraid of the spineless bullies. Fred Lassiter was only the tip of the iceberg."

"No kidding." She glanced over her shoulder again at Travers. "Where the hell does she get off even showing her face around here?"

"She feels a lot worse about this than you think."

"Yeah? And just how much do the two of you know about all this union bullshit at the plant?"

"More than you. But not enough where we can do anything about it. Until we get more concrete evidence."

Mona's sarcasm slipped out, "Unh, hunh, I'm sure Billie Travers is just busting down doors to find it, too. And what's more concrete? Harris and Springer with smoking guns? CEO Brantwell's bloody footprints?"

She stared down at the graves one last time, then whirled, walking swiftly up the hillside to the car.

Cullen started after her. "Mona!"

Mona ignored him, reached the car and climbed in.

A pitiless, steely-eyed glacier, Travers watched them from her vantage point, fascinated at what was transpiring between the two.

## 12

The club where Terri's band, The Wolves, was playing was a run-down, sleazy dive set in the triangular nexus where Devil's River, Santa Mira and Glen Cove met. Guitarist Juana and two others pulled up in a Volkswagen van and unloaded their gear on the sidewalk.

Mona and Terri pulled up in their car, and Mona slid behind the wheel as Terri got out. Terri leaned down, not shutting the door. She reached over and switched off the ignition.

"Hey, c'mon, why don't you stick around. The show's early because it's Sunday. We can have a drink together at the bar before they open."

Mona looked away

"Don't worry about Mama. She's okay by herself. C'mon, it'll do you good."

Mona nodded and reluctantly joined her, walking with Terri, and following the band as they carried their equipment into the bar.

Merle sat on the sofa in the Anderson living room. A .44 Magnum lay on the coffee table along with a scale, various paraphernalia and two ounces of heroin. He worked carefully, preoccupied, with a delicate touch and precision that seemed out of character.

There was a low thumping from down the hall, and he immediately got up to investigate. Merle opened the door to Consuela's bedroom. She turned over fitfully, then was still, fast asleep. Merle closed the door.

Loud music blasted from the nightclub jukebox. Mona downed a shot of bourbon. Terri sat bored at the bar watching the rest of her band-mates set their equipment up on stage. Mona gestured to the bartender who set up another, and she immediately upended that one, too. An over-the-top garage band song blasted from the PA, and Mona turned her attention to fiery, petite Juana as she jumped onto the dance floor to rock out. Suddenly the club's sound guy flipped on a strobe light. Mona downed one more shot, then leapt up and started gyrating next to the dancing girl.

The rest of the band and bar employees paid scant attention, but Terri was surprised and intrigued at Mona's letting go. Suddenly after twenty or thirty seconds of rocking out, Mona put her hands over her mouth and bolted from the floor towards the restrooms in back. One of the band on stage laughed.

Mona dropped to her knees on the grimy floor before the toilet and puked. She coughed and gagged. Gradually her fit subsided, and she stood, plunging her face down next to the lone faucet in the dirty sink. Turning the spigot, she let it bath her face, took some into her mouth, then spit it out.

She came out of the restroom, paused, woozy and drunk, tried to get her bearings, then turned and left through the side exit. Bursting through the door, she didn't notice Cullen in plainclothes, standing against the alley wall. He put his cigarette out beneath his heel and grabbed her arm as she passed.

"Hey!"

She angrily yanked herself free from his grasp.

"What do you want?"

"I want to talk to you."

"Well, *I don't* want to talk to *you*."

"You're drunk."

She turned back to reenter the club, but once more he grabbed her arm. This time she spontaneously slammed into him, kissing him hard on the lips. He pushed her away, a bit surprised. There was only a couple of seconds before they were once more in each others' arms, this time totally surrendering to a passionate embrace.

The club was now letting in customers. It wasn't a huge crowd, but there were at least twenty people milling about on the dance floor. A couple were punk rockers, but most were very young, male working class stiffs. The band started to play, ripping into their music with abandon. Surprisingly, Terri was a consummate performer, alternately shouting, whispering and singing, almost crooning at times.

Out in the alley behind the club, dusk was starting to enfold Cullen and Mona. The descending darkness made her feel enveloped in a fog of needy affection and confused regrets, and she pulled out of their clench. They looked into each other's eyes for almost a full minute before Mona pushed herself away from him. For the first time, she became aware it was Terri's band that was thundering away inside. She turned from Cullen and rested her forehead against the opposite wall.

"I don't know why I did that."

"I'm glad you did."

"Yeah, well, I don't know if I am."

The muffled band's song ended as Mona glanced over her shoulder at him. Another song started right away, and she thrust herself away from the wall, then opened the rear exit and disappeared inside. Cullen stared at the door, then down at his feet.

As still drunk Mona stumbled in, she was nearly blindsided by an even drunker punk slamming his way around the room. She skillfully dodged him, then took up a position near the bar to watch her sister's spectacle.

Near the end of the song, Terri, having trouble, glared at the drummer and then, Juana, the guitarist. Right before the song ended, Terri angrily kicked over the snare drum. The rest of the band chaotically finished the song as a fistfight erupted between Terri and the drummer. The bass player, a long-haired guy in glam type threads, yanked Terri away. She lurched offstage, followed by Juana. Catcalls welled up out of the audience.

Mona shook her head in disgust.

Terri exploded out the front door and down the sidewalk, shadowed by Juana. A few fans straggled out, halfheartedly following them.

"Hey, Terri." A drunken male groupie called out.

Terri stopped abruptly, whirled, ignoring Juana and ready to rip the fan's head off.

"Get back in that rathole and don't fuckin' follow me!"
The kid seemed crushed and, severely deflated, meekly followed her instructions.

Terri suddenly noticed Juana.

"What-the-fuck do you want?"

"What's wrong? Why did you do that?"

Terri, feeling superior, was incredulous. "What is wrong? What is fucking wrong! For starters, a shitty ass drummer who doesn't know what the fuck dynamics are.

"C'mon, Terri, he was playing okay."

"Look who's talking. You couldn't tell a good drummer if one fell on top of you. Plus you want to know what else was wrong?"
Juana was too scared to ask.

"You. You suck. You can't play guitar worth shit. Don is always covering for you onstage having to play his bass twice as much, propping you up 'cause you drink hard liquor before we play."

Juana turned to walk back into the club, but Terri reached out, violently grabbing her.

"Hey, don't walk away when I'm talking to you."

She didn't know her own strength because Juana lost her balance, landing on her ass, and she began to cry. Terri was suddenly silent and backed away a step, realizing she had gone too far. She softened, seeing her friend in pain.

She leaned down to help her but, as she reached for Juana's arm, a syringe fell out of her top pocket and landed on the sidewalk. Juana wiped her tears with one hand and picked up the rig with the other, studying it.

Mona emerged from the club, but stopped and watched the scene from a distance.

Juana looked up at Terri. "Goddamn you. You're talking to me about drinking. You told all of us you weren't shooting dope anymore."

Juana threw the rig at a sheepish, chastened Terri as she picked herself up from the concrete. It landed in the gutter. The petite guitarist dusted herself off, then stormed back towards the club.
Terri called out, "Juana."

Juana didn't look back, instead throwing up her right hand behind her to flip Terri off. As she passed Mona, she whispered hoarsely, "Your sister sucks."

## 13

Merle was still at work in the Anderson living room but had numerous little bags of dope finished. He mopped his brow with the back of his hand. There was a noise again, and he turned.

"What the –?"

Consuela stood in the hall entrance, strangely defiant and charged with strength. "What are you doing here, you filthy scum?"

"Well, well, well. Hi, Mom. How are we doin' today? Up and around, hunh? The hypochondriac gig's getting boring?"

"Terri's going to tell you she doesn't want to see you anymore."

He gave her a wicked smile, "Is that right? Somehow I think you jumped your track a bit."

Consuela coughed out her next tirade. "You-you-son-of-a-bitch!" She picked up the huge fifties end table lamp and threw it at him, but he jumped, sidestepped and it missed, crashing instead into the TV set.

Merle's fake good humor gave way to full-blooded anger. "You ole bitch. Get the fuck out of here before you start losing me money!"

Consuela spotted the white powder on the table. "What are you doing? Here in my house?"

Merle circled her, smiling. "You got alot of guts, Mom."

She edged away from him, bumped into the sofa end table and picked up a slender vase. "You bastard. You're just like him."

In spite of his anger, Merle's curiosity got the better of him, "Who?"

"My dead husband."

Merle snorted with laughter. "You mean Terri's daddy, Pete?" He jumped towards her, she sidestepped, and he fell across a footstool. She bashed the vase down towards his head, but he was too fast for her, and she missed again. He grabbed both of her arms and pulled her down on top of him. They wrestled on the floor for a few seconds, and he managed to roll her over beneath him.

"You just bought yourself a one-way ticket." He laughed again and gave her a hard right to the jaw. Unexpectedly, she brought the vase down on his left temple. He collapsed on top of her, stunned. She struggled like a hellcat beneath him, coughing all the while. Blood trickling from his scalp, he grabbed a pillow from the couch and slipped it over her face. He shifted all his weight on top of it, and her thrashing became even more violent. Soon the frantic motion of her limbs subsided. He smiled, slipped the cushion off of her face and placed it back on the couch. Grabbing hold of both her wrists, he dragged her into the hall and down to her room. A throw rug bunched under her, and he impatiently kicked at it. He ripped back the rumpled sheets on her bed, picked her up and heaved her lifeless corpse onto the mattress. Nervous and tense, he gingerly pulled aside the window curtains and looked outside.

The neighborhood was still, quiet.

Merle glared back down at the dead Consuela as he snatched a washcloth from the nightstand and mopped his bloody scalp.

He hurried into the living room and began straightening it up, picking up the pieces of the broken lamp and the vase. Luckily, the TV was unharmed. Quickly, he swept up the loose heroin powder with an index card into a large plastic baggie, threw the couple handfuls of balloons into another baggie, and that was when he heard it, the sound of a car pulling into the drive. He paused for just a second, then threw the baggies and the scale into a small canvas satchel. He dashed back down the hall to Mona and Terri's bedroom, then returned just as the girls walked in.

Mona gave him a disgusted look as she spotted him.

"What-the-hell is he doing here?"

Terri put her hands on her hips defiantly. "I told him he could come over. He had to make some phone calls. His phone got disconnected."

Merle gave them both a twisted smile. "I like you, too, Mona."

She ignored his jibe. "Terri, you know the way Mama feels about him."

"So? She's asleep." She glanced uncertainly at Merle for confirmation, "Right?"

Merle put on his best innocent expression. "I dunno. I guess so. I haven't seen hide nor hair of her.

Mona stormed down the hall to Consuela's room.

Terri lowered her voice, "Goddamn it, Merle. I thought you told me you were gonna be gone by the time we got back." He sat down on the couch, staring at his hands, twiddling his grimy thumbs. Terri looked on the bright side, "Well, at least you didn't have all that shit spread out all over the place when we walked in."

Mona's muffled voice rang out. "Terri."

"What now?"

"Come here, quick!"

Terri made a face at Merle and walked briskly down the hall.

Mona sat on the edge of the bed, Consuela's body cradled in her arms. She gently slapped Consuela's cheeks but there was no response. Terri suddenly was very worried. Her voice sounded like a little girl's, "What's wrong?"

Mona didn't answer, placing her ear to Consuela's chest. She listened for about twenty seconds, then sat up straight, her face drained of blood. She felt Consuela's wrist for a pulse. Terri put her hands to her mouth. "Oh, Mona. No."

Mona turned to her. "She's gone, Terri." Mona stood up, rattled but determined. "Merle!"

A few seconds ticked by, then he casually ambled in, lazily stopped and leaned against the doorjam.

"What?"

Mona pointed at Consuela. "What do you know about this?"

Merle seemed genuinely bewildered. "What?"

"Mama's dead."

Terri was beside herself. Mona came up close, only inches

away from Merle's unshaven face. "What do you know about this, you bastard?"

Right then, Cullen happened to be driving by the house in his unmarked cruiser when he spotted Merle's pickup outside and slowed to a stop. He reached for his radio mike.

"This is Cullen. Come in –"

The Sheriff dispatcher answered, "– this is base, Detective Cullen. Go ahead."

"Have just spotted what may be the convenience store homicide suspect's pickup outside 9234 East Van Doren. Send back-up."

Cullen got out of the car, walked to the front door and knocked. After a few seconds, Mona opened it.

She was surprised, "Hello, Officer Cullen. Just the man I wanted to see. Come in."

She closed the door behind him as he followed her, and she off-handedly wiped the tears from her cheeks with one hand. With her turned, Cullen didn't notice her agitated state.

"Whose truck is that out there?"

"Truck?...it's Merle Chambers'...he's back here."

Cullen removed his gun from his shoulder holster as he fell in line behind Mona. He reached out to grab her and then moved to take the lead.

"What –?"

Merle already had his .44 drawn and cocked. Terri glanced up from Consuela's body.

"What're you doing, Merle?"

"Shut up!"

Cullen cautiously ventured into the doorway, and Merle squeezed off a deafening shot that splintered the doorjam. Terri hit the floor as Cullen responded in kind, exploding the bedside lamp. The room was plunged into shadow. Merle grabbed Consuela's corpse and propped it up in front of him as a shield just as Cullen let loose again.

Mona, watching from behind Cullen, called out, "No!"

Two bullets ripped through lifeless flesh. The force sent Merle toppling back with Consuela, shattering the window and through it. Cullen regained his feet and raced to the opening. Consuela's body lay crumpled and contorted, her arms and head bent at an awkward ankle over the outside windowsill. Merle was clumsily running to his pickup. Cullen squeezed off two more shots but missed. Merle fired the engine, slammed the truck into gear, roared out onto the road, then careened away in a cloud of dust and exhaust.

Inside the house, Mona switched on the hall light. Shaken to her core, she stumbled to the window. Cullen had climbed outside, and Mona was visibly shaking as she gently helped him lift Consuela back into the room, then return her wrecked body to the bed. Mona was doing her best not to cry as Cullen climbed in and holstered his gun.

"Who was that?"

"Terri's boyfriend," her voice sounded drained, zombie-like, "Merle Chambers."

Mona and Cullen trailed behind Terri as she stumbled into the living room with a blank stare and plopped down onto the couch. Once again, Mona tried to stifle her weeping, but this time she was unsuccessful. Cullen put his arm around her.

There was sound of sirens wailing from several blocks away, then cars screeching to a stop on the Anderson home's front lawn. Sheriff Billie Travers and Deputies Jerry and Tom hurried into the room, their hands on their holstered weapons.

Travers was all business. "Where is he?"

Cullen replied sheepishly, "He got away...he killed their mother."

Terri came out of her daze, "She was already dead. From the TB."

Travers was getting frustrated, "Just who is this guy? And why was he here?

Mona felt her gorge rising. She wasn't sure why, but she suddenly couldn't stand the sight of Travers there in her own living room, lording it over them. Somehow, she managed to keep her voice stoic, "He's Terri's boyfriend."

Cullen butted in, "His name is Merle Chambers."

"I see…" Travers spotted something under the coffee table "...what's this?"

She stooped, then picked up one of the tiny bags of heroin that Merle had missed. She used a fingernail to make a hole, then licked her powdered finger. "Just what I thought."

Terri's head sank. Mona stared at her in disbelief. Anger took the place of her grief. "What-the-fuck is that shit doing here?"

Terri couldn't answer.

Travers gestured to one of her deputies, "Jerry, I want this place searched from top to bottom..." She glanced at Terri, "Especially this young lady's bedroom."

Deputy Tom came back into the living room. "Sheriff, the old lady's dead all right."

Travers nodded, "Okay, Tom, go ahead and call the morgue for Mrs. Anderson."

She saw an opening to get at Mona and slinked into it, "And you, don't play dumb. You ought to know that your sister is down in our files as an habitual user."

Knowing his boss all too well, alarm bells were going off in Cullen's head, "Now wait a minute, Billie. You don't think Mona had anything to do with –"

"John, I don't know what to think. But I'm taking both these 'model' citizens in for some further questioning, maybe charges. I just don't know."

Cullen was flustered. "Billie, you know...you at least know Mona didn't have anything to do with that stuff? Or the convenience store killing?"

"I don't know any such thing, John. And I'd appreciate it if you didn't fall all over yourself trying to tell me how to do my job."

Mona couldn't believe her ears. Terri was getting very worried.

"What convenience store killing?"

"Don't play the innocent one with me, missy. You know damn well that your boyfriend was the one who killed the Fromkiss boy who worked at the all night market."

"What?"

Cullen rubbed his forehead in frustration, "Billie, I think you're –"

"No, I'm not jumping to any conclusions. Better to be safe than sorry."

Deputy Jerry came back into the living room with Merle's canvas satchel in one hand and a baggie full of pills and syringes in the other.

"Found these under one of the beds in the back bedroom."

Mona shot an angry look at Terri. Travers whistled and smiled, daintily taking the baggie between her fingers.

"Is that so?"

A knock sounded at the open front door and two men from the coroner's office barged in. "Where's the stiff?"

Travers hooked her thumb over her shoulder towards the hall. Mona raced after the two men as they headed for Consuela's bedroom.

## 14

John Cullen was alone in Sherif Billie Travers' office, and he paced impatiently to and fro. The door flew open, and a hyper Travers raced to her desk, sitting, and simultaneously picking up the phone.

"Madge, give me the Stockton sheriff –"

Cullen reached over and pressed down the receiver button, hanging it up.

His face was red with anger. "Just a minute, Billie. You're going to take a few minutes and talk to me. You know I've been waiting for over two hours, and I'm damn well not going to wait any longer."

Travers couldn't believe her ears. "You're acting kind of tired of your job, John. Correct me if I'm wrong. I don't appreciate anybody talking to me that way, especially one of my former deputies who just recently, I might add, got promoted to detective. And you hanging up the phone for me. That wasn't too polite, John. I've got three separate emergencies on my hands."

"I want Mona Anderson released and the charges against her dropped. And I'm not asking you, I'm telling you.

"Sorry, John," Travers kept her cool, "No can do. First of all, I don't like being ordered around. That's why I'm the sheriff. Second, I'm not so sure Mona wasn't in on all this. She had a wild past before she decided to straighten out and fly right a few years ago. It's obvious her sister was partnering with Chambers, and I'm holding both of them – Mona and Terri – over for arraignment. Possession of narcotics and narcotics paraphernalia, accessory to armed robbery, accessory to murder. And that is final."

"Murder of who? Fromkiss?"

"Their old lady. The autopsy confirmed my suspicions. Beaten and suffocated."

"Christ."

"Don't act so goddamn shocked."

"That's final, hunh?"

"That's final."

Cullen ripped his badge from his inside pocket and tossed it in the trash can beside the desk.

Travers suppressed a grin, "Looks like we've got a lovesick public servant on our hands."

"Fuck you, Billie."

"Anytime."

The remark made him want to slap her, but he restrained himself. "With Harris and Springer's people on their jury, those girls won't have a chance. And you know you've got something personal against Mona because of the Rose Martin thing. And me. So fuck you."

He stormed out. Travers fished the badge out of the trash, brushed it off and laughed softly.


There was a kind of stunned silence in the courtroom. Even the usual whispering one might hear immediately before a verdict was absent. Holly Harris and Steve Springer sat poker-faced beside the blithely ambivalent Billie Travers. On the defendants' side of the room, Cullen and teacher Millie Shaw sat beside each other, with Mel Dempsey behind them, stone sober. Cullen was stoic, but Millie was filled with apprehension.

Mona and Terri sat side-by-side, an obviously explosive but stifled anger on their faces. Terri did not look well, sweating profusely with her red thatch of hair matted down.

Springer leaned over and whispered in Harris' ear.

"A diet of cold turkey doesn't agree with the white trash Anderson."

"Damn junkie. She would have to be Merle Chamber's woman."

The jury foreman stood up and faced the taciturn judge. "Have you reached a verdict?"

"Yes, your honor. We find the defendant Teresa Anderson guilty on one count of accessory to armed robbery and guilty on one count of accessory to second degree murder."

Terri's and Mona's faces went ashen.

"We find the defendant Mona Anderson guilty on one count of accessory to armed robbery and guilty on one count of obstructing justice."

Mona and Terri looked at each other as if it was what they expected. Mona took a sidelong glance at their smartly coiffed, pant-suited Vogue model of a lawyer. She meekly stared down at her sheaf of documents.

Millie started to quietly weep.

Harris and Springer smiled casually at Travers. The judge acknowledged the verdict.

"Inasmuch as I feel that this matter should be expedited as soon as possible to perhaps aid in affecting the capture of the principal armed robbery and murder suspect, Merle Chambers, I shall ask the prisoners to rise...I shall impose sentence without further delay."

Mona and Terri stood up.

"Mona and Teresa Anderson your narcotics cases will be disposed of at a later date. Have either one of you anything to say before I impose sentence regarding the matter before us today?"

Terri shook her head, but Mona nodded.

"Yes, your honor." She paused dramatically. "When will Holly Harris and Steven Springer be indicted and brought to trial for the murder of Phillip Martin?"

Harris and Springer turned beet-red as the court erupted. The judge gaveled, banging repeatedly on his desk, until he had brought the unruly court to order.

He ignored Mona's inflammatory question.

"Teresa and Mona Anderson you have been found guilty as charged on one count each of accessory to armed robbery. Teresa Anderson, you have also been found guilty of accessory to second degree murder of Consuela Anderson. I hereby sentence you to fifteen years at the women's prison at Tehachapi. Mona Anderson, you have also been found guilty of obstructing justice. I sentence you to five years at the same institution."

He pounded his gavel again. "This court is now adjourned."

Mona glanced at Cullen and Millie as she was led behind Terri out of the courtroom.

Merle was curled up in a ball in the unmade cot of his broiling Airstream trailer home. Empty liquor bottles and take-out containers littered the floor. He spread out the newspaper in front of him and read the story of Terri's and Mona's conviction all over again. A crazy look on his face, Merle started talking to the photo of Terri. He poked the newspaper with a greasy finger.

"Don't you fret, Terri. You ain't gonna be in that joint too long. No sir, no sir."

Cullen waited behind a massive screen in the visiting room. A door opened, and Mona appeared with a guard. She wafted over opposite Cullen and plopped down on a rickety metal stool bolted to the floor.

"Hi."

"Hi, yourself. Thanks for coming to see me. I didn't realize you'd left the force until I saw you in the courtroom. Terri told me. I guess she heard it through the grapevine."

Cullen felt embarrassed, awkward. "I'm doing all I can for you. I've talked to my cousin in San Francisco. His best friend is this high-powered lawyer. He's very interested in your case...for mercenary reasons. But he's such a barracuda, it'd be a real plus to have him on your side for the appeal."

"Yeah? Thanks..."

They were both at a loss for words.

"...I guess you know that they're shipping us out this afternoon?"

Cullen was so upset he was afraid to talk.

"John Cullen, you know what I don't get?"

He shook his head.

"Why you're doing all this for me."

He hesitated. "I suppose you know how I feel about you. It kind of crept up on me, then hit me over the head. But with this whole scam from Harris and Springer, and Travers' frame, I'd've done it for anyone."

Mona looked at him stoicly.

"They've sent the papers on a wild goose chase, bought judge and jury. They're afraid of you, but there's more to it than that. Is there something else involved that you can think of ?"

Mona was puzzled, "Like what?"

"I don't know. Could it have anything to do with Terri and Merle?"

"I – I...No, I don't see how...why?"

"Mel Dempsey mentioned to me that he saw Merle talking to Holly Harris."

Mona was shocked.

Cullen changed the subject. "To tell you the truth, I'm worried that these bastards could arrange to do you in the place you're going. You'll have to watch yourself every minute. You and Terri stick together."

"Terri and I have already got all that figured out. We're going to be watching each others' backs.

Cullen wanted to say more, not let her go, but he was tongue-tied, frustrated by his feelings and his fear of showing her too much,

"I wish to God there was something more that I could do."

"You've done enough already, John. Believe me, I'm stronger than I look. They're going to have to crush me, grind me to dust under their big money machine before they'll ever get me to shut my trap."

Cullen smiled weakly. The guard tapped Mona on the shoulder.

"Okay, okay." She stood up, then headed for the door, but a couple paces later, in the open doorway, she turned around, smiled warmly and blew him a kiss.

## 15

The prison bus was haunted by a combination of indistinct odors, but Mona thought she smelled a powerful disinfectant trying unsuccessfully to tamp down the smells of unwashed bodies, cigarettes – not allowed actually, but a blind eye was apparently being turned – not to mention the aroma of menstrual blood and sex. Mona and Terri sat together amongst an assortment of black, Asian, Latina and Anglo women, all with a variety of hair colors and unorthodox-cum-lazy styles, which included half of them – no matter the race – having bleached blonde locks. There were even a couple of elderly females obviously in their mid-sixties.

Tex, an Asian girl with ratted black hair, pulled a lone smoke out of her shirt pocket and lit up. Terri stared at her, envy in her eyes. Tex relished the smoke.

"Um-um, fuck yeah." She noticed Mona and began to flirt, "Want a drag?"

Mona shook her head, but Terri reached out and intercepted the offered cigarette.

Tex waxed indignant. "I wasn't talking to you, girl."

Terri sucked on the butt, not replying.

Mona smiled, hoping to smooth any potentially ruffled feathers. "Let her have it. She's okay. She's my sister."

Tex was incredulous, "Yeah? I know she's no blood relation."

"She is. Same daddy."

"And what's being your sister got to do with anything? My sister is a lying, vicious cunt," Tex turned sarcastic, "But hey, I guess we're just a bunch of sisters *'doin' it for ourselves.'*"

Terri handed the smoke back to her. Tex eyed her dubiously, but started bragging,

"You know, I can really appreciate the taste of good tobacco. My mama used to work in a cigar factory in Cuba. Handmade. The real thing. Smoked my first at the age of six."

"Yeah?"

Mona was oblivious to their pissing contest, but Terri was fascinated by Tex.

Tex warmed to the subject. "Unh, hunh, sure, sure, honey. I love cigars. I'll take a cigar over a cigarette anytime...when I can get 'em."

Debbie, a chunky, bleached blonde Latina seated on the other side of Tex, nudged her. "Bitch, don't be so stingy with the coffin nails."

Tex cackled, "Debbie, you crack me up. Here, you need this more than me –" She handed her the disappearing butt, "– knock yourself out."

Debbie grabbed it, inhaled and greedily sucked up the vapors.

They finally reached the Tehachapi facilty. The prison bus pulled into the fenced enclosure, stopped with a lurch, and the prisoners started filing out.

Once night fell and the lights were out, Mona sank down on her turf, the bottom half of a bunk bed. Debbie, her cellmate, nervously paced.

"Shit. Shit!"

Mona did not look up.

"My lawyer said it'd never get this far."

"That should teach you something about lawyers."

"Don't think I don't know it, honey. But what choice did I have? The fucking pigs had me dead to rights."

Mona feigned interest, "Yeah?"

"My pimp with a six inch gash in his throat and a straight razor with my prints."

Mona turned over and stared at the wall. Debbie laughed at her reaction.

"Yeah, yeah, I know about you." Debbie became even more sarcastic, "You got a real raw deal, right? First time, hunh? Accessory, and everybody says it's your sis's fault. Hey, that's life."

Terri sat cross-legged on the floor. Her cellmate Tex had her hands on her hips and stared down at her with disgust. "What're you doin' down there on the floor. You look like a damn hippie."

"Don't bug me, bitch."

"What did you say?" Tex bent down and stared Terri in the eye.

"You heard me, Tex. Fuck off!"

"You're lucky I like you. I cut up bitches with mouths ain't even half as big as yours."

"Start cuttin', honey! I'm a tangled-up, pussy-cuttin' motherfucker since the day I was born. I'll tie you in goddamn knots if you start feelin' yer oats."

Tex glared at her in disbelief. Terri looked up at her and smiled.

Grey dawn light filtered through a barred window at the end of the long hall. Twenty bedraggled inmates in blue denim attire were lined up, ten against either wall. Candice, a petite wiry guard with a clipboard, strolled down between the two rows of restless females. She bit obsessively at the end of her pencil.

"Okay, that wasn't so hard, now was it? But just so you gals don't think we don't have anything harder planned for you than you remembering your names at five o'clock in the morning –" She smiled, "Just so you don't get the wrong goddamn idea, well, I've got a little work detail all lined-up for you."

A few groans welled up from the ranks.

"I thought you'd appreciate that. I stayed up real late last night putting the finishing touches on this. I wanted to arrange things based on what I know about you individually."

Debbie, in line next to Terri, Mona and Tex, snickered. Candice looked her way but said nothing. She moved down the hall.

"Okay, Smith, Marsha-kitchen; York, Sharon-laundry; Harris, Nellie-potato field; Furstenberg, Kara-potato field; Emily, Mary-laundry...Shut up back there!" Candice shot a poisonous glance back from whence she came, then reluctantly returned to her work call. "Vondas, Latisha-potato field, Anderson, Mona-potato field; Hark, Texas-potato field; Anderson, Terri-potato field; Zapata, Debbie-laundry –"

Debbie couldn't keep her mouth shut. "Laundry! What-the-fuck! Why aren't I in the potato fields, too?"

Candice rushed up to Debbie, pushed the palm of her hand against the girl's face, catching her off-balance and sending her back-wards to the floor.

"'Cause I say so, you uppity bitch! I want to keep you and Tex separated. You two are troublemakers when you get together."

Debbie grimaced nastily, picked herself up and dusted herself off. Candice continued back down the hall with the opposite line.

Debbie whispered to Terri, "That cunt is sure gonna get hers."

Mona began to have a weird sense of déjà vu, not explicit, not too vivid, more vague, like she was somehow transported back in time to the Devil's River drive-in, the lone movie exhibition place in town, not only watching but living in one of those women-in-prison machete-maidens-in-the-Philippines exploitation pictures that some now hotshot new director had started their career on. She would not have thought it possible and felt most straight people in the nine-to-five world would have pooh-poohed the idea of prison, especially for women, actually being like that; scoffed at the idea that those movies were somehow – sometimes – accurate pictures of what went on behind bars for the fairer sex in real life. In fact, as straight arrow as she herself had become – what with trying to remove her tattoos, amongst other concessions to "society" – Mona would have been one of them not believing it. No way women's prison life could be, well, so stupid, so crazy, so gratuitously violent. But here she was in so-called real life, in a women's prison.

And it felt distinctly as if she was in an exploitation movie.

## 16

Cullen hated going back into the department but he didn't want to leave a trace of his presence behind. It made him physically ill just to look at the one story, cinder block building. He had had only a couple of friends in his division, Alex and Helen, detectives, too, but they were down in Los Angeles on two unrelated cases.

He steeled himself and pushed open the smeary glass double doors. The receptionist, Erin, was not at the front, so Cullen started to make his way unmolested through the warren of cubicles, then the first corridor. He walked laconically, almost unbearably depressed, but determined not to show it. From habit, he stopped to look through the soundproofed one-way window into the interrogation room. Travers and the prisoner, Bettina Jones, sat talking. Travers passed something bulky in a sealed manila envelope across the long table to the wicked-looking girl.

Cullen thought nothing of it, and he continued around the next corner to his former office. Deputy Jerry sat at his old desk, and he was surprised to see Cullen.

"Well, look what the cat drug in."

Short, buff Jerry, who resembled a skinny pit bull, was Travers' personal lapdog, and Cullen couldn't stand him.

Cullen tried unsuccessfully to keep the coldness out of his voice.

"I just came for that box with the last of my stuff."

Jerry grimaced and hooked his thumb over his shoulder at the cabinet against the wall. Cullen picked the box off the top of it then turned back to the corridor. He paused.

"Who's the girl in with Travers?"

Jerry smiled, "Oh, that's Bettina. A real little badass. Her and her homey, Lucy, are headed up to Tehachapi. Going to be cellmates of your pal, Mona."

Cullen vaguely nodded, but made no further comment and left. Jerry's grin widened.

The prison potato field was painfully cold. Everyone's breath nearly crystallized with the near freezing temperature as they exhaled from the monotonous task. Mona put her back into her hoeing. A few yards away, Terri lazily performed the same function. Tex stopped for a moment, wiped her brow with her shirt sleeve in spite of the chill, then rested her chin and arm on the hoe handle top. Terri glanced at her, and Tex gestured at Mona.

"She really your sister?"

"Yup. Half-sister."

"She sure is quiet. Doesn't seem like she was cut from the same cloth as you."

Terri's bitterness crept out into the open with her sarcastic tone. "That's 'cause she's educated. She's a schoolteacher." Her voice turned serious. "But you should see her when she gets started. She's as straight as an arrow now, but she can handle herself." Terri grinned, "You dig her, don't you? Want to get a taste of that pussy."

Tex didn't answer at first and started hoeing again. Ruminating on Terri's vulgar suggestion, she clucked her tongue, "Shit. girl, talking nasty stuff like that about your own kin."

The bar was a working class hellhole, but Cullen and Millie had decided to drink there anyway, for sentimental reasons. It reminded them of their time right out of high school when they both had used fake IDs to buy liquor at the less than proper watering hole. They sat at the cushioned counter, nursing shots of whiskey and waters. Cullen thought it was strange that he had been friends with Millie Shaw, but had not known either Mona or Terri. He had gotten shit back in the day, from both people he knew as well as Millie's family, for being friends with her, because she was black.

"Mona and Terri didn't move here till you were already gone to Berkeley."

That made sense. Cullen looked at her thoughtfully but made no comment.

Besides the redheaded bartender named Tommy, who had been the owner for twenty years, there were only three other men scattered in the dimness.

"So. What are you going to do for money now?"

"Now that I've made the chivalrous and impotent gesture of quitting the department?"

She smiled and nodded.

"I don't know. I haven't given it much thought. I've got about two months' back pay coming, and vacation pay, that kind of thing. And Sally Hayes over at the River Gazette said I could have my old typesetting job back. Except they're going to be upgrading from the old system next year. So I've got to eventually learn to do it on computer."

"The modern age is upon us. But that isn't hard. Used to be in the newspaper business, hunh?"

"If you can call The River Gazette a newspaper. I started there when I dropped out of Berkeley. I thought you knew."

She shook her head. "Johnny, how did you ever end up a cop?"

"I used to be pretty close to Billie Travers' dad before he died. You remember him? He was the sheriff in Devil's River for a long, long time. He was kind of a second father to me after my folks passed away. I always looked up to him. He had this quality. Like Henry Fonda in *My Darling Clementine* –"

"I didn't see it."

A noise outside distracted him, and he felt a vague sense of unease. "He played Wyatt Earp –"

A half drunk Billie Travers and Deputy Jerry stumbled into the bar. They were out of uniform and obviously off-duty.

Cullen and Millie just looked at each other. Travers and Jerry sidled up to the counter a few stools away, not yet noticing Cullen.

Millie wanted to get out of there and, in pretense, glanced at her watch. "Um, I had no idea it was this late. I've got to get up to teach children how to add and subtract tomorrow morning."

As she got up to leave and bussed Cullen on the cheek, Jerry caught sight of them.

"Hey, Billie. Look who it is. Ex-detective John Cullen. With a new dusky girlfriend."

Cullen overheard the remark and frowned. Millie patted him on the shoulder,

"I hate to leave you alone in the lion's den –"

"It's okay, Millie. Thanks. I'll see you soon."

Millie gave the new customers a dirty look as she left.

Travers and Jerry were quiet for a moment, glancing at each other and suppressing laughter. Then Travers got up, making her way towards Cullen. Just before she reached him, Cullen got up and moved to a booth.

Four or five booths away, towards the back of the bar, a lone man sat nursing a beer with his back to everyone else. No one noticed that it was Merle Chambers, quietly taking all of it in.

Travers shook her head and smiled ruefully. She noticed the jukebox at the end of the counter and theatrically sauntered over to it. She studied the selection for a few seconds. Finding a tune, she glanced over her shoulder towards Cullen then back to the jukebox. She inserted her coins and pressed a button.

A torchy, R&B-flavored rock ballad by The Bell Rays came on, with the lyrics *"Your mama's in jail now/leaving you all alone..."*

Cullen sipped his drink, staring straight ahead and not saying a word. The song continued for half a minute or so before Cullen casually rose and walked over to the jukebox. He crouched, staring pointedly at Travers as he reached behind the machine and yanked the plug. The music suddenly, jarringly went dead.

Jerry snorted. "Guess he's not a music fan."

Travers and Cullen locked stares as Cullen straightened up.

"I was ready to let bygones be bygones, water under the bridge. Everyone loses their temper once in a while. But not you, John." She shook her head again, "You just won't let it go."

Jerry nastily added, "Let *her* go."

Merle was laughing quietly to himself, drinking in the shadows.

Cullen lackadaisically moved past Travers and Jerry and headed for the door.

"You sure have changed, John."

Cullen stopped, "Billie, you're the one who's changed." He turned and walked out.

Travers swiveled around to the bar counter, shaken in spite of herself.

"Shithead. Who-the-fuck does he –"

"Shut up, Jerry." Travers downed her shot.

## 17

The house was dark, cold and lonely. Cullen wearily climbed the few steps to his back door. He switched on the light in the kitchen and set down a small bag of groceries. He pulled out a loaf of rye bread, two cans of tuna, a jar of mayonnaise, a bunch of celery, then a quart bottle of whiskey. He twisted open the bottle, took a long pull then set it on the sink as he turned attention to the tuna. Clumsily, in a fog, he opened it. Originally he was going to make tuna salad, but he was so famished, he hungrily forked some into his mouth. Putting it down, he took another swig of the quart.

He bleakly studied himself in the mirror over the sink. The water stuttered noisily as he twisted the cold spigot. He bent down, using both hands to rub water over his face and neck. When he straightened up, he found he was not alone. Merle Chambers' demented face returned his stare from the glass.

Merle had his .44 tucked snugly into the small of Cullen's back. He picked up the bottle, took a hefty gulp, but his crazy eyes never left Cullen's gaze.

"Don't mind if I do...aahhh, that's good! Good stuff for an ex-cop. You selling futures on what's down the line for you, Cullen?"

Merle found his own sarcasm very funny.

Cullen shifted his weight a little, saying nothing. Merle's good humor disappeared.

"Watch it, detective. I got my spinal cracker aimed right where it'll do the most good."

Both were quiet for almost thirty seconds.

"What do you want?"

"Same thing you want. To be left alone – with me and my girl. That's it, ain't it, Johnny boy? Why you left the valiant force? Because of Mona, that mocha-colored, high-and-mighty cunt?"

Cullen just stared at him.

"Her being half Mex? That doesn't bother you?" He was genuinely curious and, for a few seconds, his malice all but disappeared, looking for the key to something, some idea what constituted humanity, so maybe he could turn the lock for himself and get in, steal the compassion and tolerance and affection to exorcise his own poison. But just as quickly, it was gone again, a whispering, taunting phantom that teased him and mocked his emotional blankness – his impotence. "Yeah, and me? I kind of miss her sis, Terri. Looks like we got something in common, whether we like it or not. Well, don't we?" Merle gave him a good poke in the kidneys and clenched his teeth. "Well, don't we?"

Cullen was still stoic.

"Playing your cards close? It doesn't matter. I know. It's in your face, your lousy, self-righteous kisser. That's good. That's what I wanted to hear, even if I had to hear it from me." He gestured at the quart, "Grab that. C'mon, we're going to take it easy."

With his free hand, he steered Cullen into the living room, motioning him down onto the raggedy sofa with the gun. "Easy now –"

He took the quart from Cullen, bubbled it good while staring at the ex-lawman, " – so, so, so. This is workin' out fine. Us talkin' and jokin' like we known each other for years. Old pals."

Cullen looked away and stared into empty space. Merle jumped, grabbed him by the hair and jabbed the gun close up against his cheek. "Except we're not old pals, are we? And we both hate each other's guts, right? Right. Answer me, you goddamn faggot."

Cullen finally spoke, "You been doing pretty well for the both of us. Why should I start now and maybe ruin everything?"

"Oh, you're funny. But you get my point at least. And you're going to keep on gettin' it till I say otherwise."

He released Cullen and pointed at the bottle with the gun.

"Go ahead, have a drink. You need one."

Cullen took a long swallow.

"Clears your head, don't it? Keep it clear for what I'm going to tell you. I know you'd like nothin' better than to see me suckin' the gas. You're thinkin' 'I almost wish I was back on the force so I could bounce this motherfucker from here to kingdom come.' I read you like a book, Jack. But you're not going to bounce me anywhere. In fact, you're going to help me."

"Sure, sure, I'm going to help you, Merle."

"You may not think so, but you are. Believe me. I'm gettin' Terri out. Mona, too."

Cullen looked at Merle as if he was crazy.

"Yeah, you heard me right. Out. O-U-T. And you know why I'm talkin' to Mona's big strong lover boy, Johnny Cullen? No? Well, you're going to tie up some loose ends."

"You're cracked." He started to get up, but Merle slammed him back down. "Not half as cracked as you think. You see, those guys who had Phil Martin killed – well, I work for 'em sometimes. You might call it freelance work."

Cullen stared at him again.

"That's right. And they want Mona out of there. So if she starts shooting off her mouth again, there won't be nobody to listen to her. Not even other jailbirds."

"Seems like a lot of trouble. Why don't they just kill her?"

"It's too soon. Maybe down the line. But it'll look funny right now. Folks are already squawkin' about the Martin case. Travers has had Federal men breathin' down her sweaty neck. The whole labor union thing. Violation of civil rights. All that cry baby liberal stuff. She'd like nothin' better than to wash her hands of the whole thing. Her last trick for Harris and Springer was gettin' Mona sent up the river. Help destroy – what do you call it? – her credibility." He laughed. "All that stuff with me and the dope kind of worked out okay, hunh? Even if it cost me a shitload of money. Travers doesn't know about me being in with Harris and Springer, though. She'd shit a brick. She won't know about this lil' escape plot, either. She'd never ever, ever stand for it. And I'll tell you why in a minute."

"I won't lift a finger to help."

"Yeah, you will. 'Cause if you don't, Terri's going to end up a real lil' orphan girl. An only child, you might say."

"I thought that was too risky."

"Not if she's plugged tryin' to escape. If lover boy isn't there to look after her.

"But if I don't help, there won't be a prison break for Mona to get killed in."

"Wrong, bright boy. There'll still be an escape. It'll just be harder, riskier. The fact is there's a good chance Mona won't come, might even blow the whistle on this whole thing if you're not involved." He let that sink in. "I'm not just doing this job for Harris and Springer. I want Terri. I need her. You don't come into this, I'll do it the hard way. But, both you and your old lady will go down. You want to know how Mona'll get it?" Merle smiled, relishing the moment. "Billie Travers took out a contract on her."

Disbelief as well as fear spread over Cullen's features. "I don't believe you. Billie would never –"

"Oh, yeah, she would. I can see you *do* believe it, by the look on your face. Harrris and Springer wouldn't be happy if they knew. That Travers is one mean, grudge-holdin' bitch, ain't she? I even know the girl who's got the contract. A foxy Anglo *chola* named Bettina Jones."

Cullen remembered Travers passing the envelope to Bettina in the interrogation room, remembered Jerry's arrogant know-it-all words, *"Oh, that's Bettina. Her and her homey, Lucy, are headed up to Tehachapi in the next day or two. Going to be a cellmate of your pal, Mona."* He realized it was true, and it shook him to his core.

"But, let's look on the bright side, why don't we? With you in the picture, you get what you want and make things a whole lot easier. Just remember. From where I'm sittin', you don't got any choice. The clock on your bitch is already tickin'."

## 18

Terri and Debbie strolled casually side by side in the prison exercise yard where other inmates were scattered, smoking, talking. They came to a wall where eight women listened to Tex playing guitar.

"Jesus Christ, how'd she get that in here?"

"Her old man."

"What?"

"Her boyfriend, Andy. He's a fuckin' gangster. Got dough comin' out of his ass. He paid off a guard somewhere down the line."

"Nice friend to have."

"You ain't kiddin' – hey, look." Debbie pointed down a ways to a deserted section of the wall where Mona stood forlornly watching Tex. She snickered, "Your sensitive sibling."

Terri made a face and turned away.

"What's the matter, Terri? Guilty conscience?"

Terri turned back, defensive. "About what?"

Debbie became mock sheepish. "Oh, I don't know."

"What!"

"Forget it already. I didn't mean anything."

They stood there in silence for a few minutes, watching Tex.

Black-haired Bettina and blonde Lucy came out of the main building into the yard. Debbie caught sight of them and nudged Terri.

"Shit. I don't believe it."

Bettina and Lucy stopped in front of Debbie and Terri. Both cast a scornful eye on Terri.

Still, chameleon Bettina came across with a deceptively casual air. "Hi, Debbie."

"God, I don't believe you're in here. How'd they ever pin a rap on you?"

"Funny. I was wondering the same thing myself. Maybe Tex could answer that question."

Debbie glanced at Tex, then back at Bettina, puzzled.

"You don't get it? Why am I not surprised?"

"Wait a minute. You don't mean Tex –"

"You always did have to have somebody draw you a god-damn picture. I got popped the day after she was sentenced. And those pigs knew shit only a couple people knew – where I was getting' the stuff – Tex was one of them."

"What about Merle Chambers? He knew, too."

Terri looked at Debbie like she wanted to strangle her.

Merle's complicity, fueled perhaps from bitterness over the money he paid, hadn't occurred to Bettina, but it didn't fit the narrative she'd come up with, stitching a patchwork quilt of old grudges she and Tex had against each other. She shook her head vaguely and changed the subject. "Hey, you met my girl, Lucy?"

Lucy didn't acknowledge the introduction. She was staring at Tex.

Debbie betrayed her awkwardness. "Hey, glad to meet you. This is my friend, Terri. She's Tex's roomie."

Both Bettina and Lucy eyed each other, then studied Terri with a new interest.

"Hey." Terri was a master of tone, able to sound ambivalent and defiant simultaneously.

"Bunkin' with a lowdown bitch like that, you better watch yourself, honey."

Lucy felt the need to chime in, "Fuckin' A!"

Terri smirked. "I'll keep it in mind."

Bettina and Lucy cracked smiles.

Bettina could make anyone she pleased feel uncomfortable with only a few words, so she tried her intimidating demeanor on Terri.

"You're Mona Anderson's sister, am I right?"

"So?"

"Another lowdown bitch can't keep her mouth shut."

Terri saw red but didn't respond.

The pair walked slowly off together.

Debbie was worried. "Shit, there's going to be trouble now. Especially with Tex bringin' in that stuff through Andy."

"What stuff?'

Debbie got agitated at Terri's fake naivete and grabbed her with both hands by the crook of her left arm, exposing gnarly track marks.

"C'mon, Terri, don't play dumb with me. Everybody in here knows you have a habit."

Terri wrenched her arm free, "Really? I guess you and your friends aren't as stupid as you look." She gave Debbie a withering stare, then strolled quickly away.

Cullen laid on the couch, smoking and listening to a song from the MC5 album *High Time* on the old-fashioned console stereo. The TV was on, too, but the image rolled in vertical hold instability. He wearily closed his eyes.

The song continued for another twenty seconds or so, then was cut off with the rasp of the tone arm needle scratching vinyl. He jumped into a sitting position to find Merle in front of the stereo, his back turned and studying a framed photo on the wall over the fireplace. Merle laughed, grabbed the picture and turned around.

"Motherfuck. You got to be kiddin' me."

Merle flashed the framed photo of an early 1970s student demonstration on the Berkeley campus. He pointed at a figure in the foreground in the front lines. "That's you, right?" He tossed the picture in Cullen's lap.

"What were you, Cullen, a goddamn student radical? You and Phil Martin would've *loooved* each others' asses. What a douchebag you are. You're the kind of prick gave my daddy nightmares the last couple years he was around, right before he shuffled off to Buffalo."

Cullen didn't look at the picture, just took hold of it and set it on the edge of the sofa.

Merle picked up a stack of books from over the fireplace and started to read out the titles, "*Das Kapital: A Psycho-Sexual Analysis, Tap Roots of Fascism, Archetypes of Totalitarian Plunder, The Rat on Fire, Misogynists vs. Miscegenators, Blood Ritual in Western Religion*…Christ, you sure like to complicate your life, don't you? Why do it? I don't understand half these words. What-the-fuck? A bunch of elitist pricks talking in a foreign language."

Suddenly Merle stretched out his left arm and swept all of Cullen's books off the mantelpiece, sending them flying across the room's broadloom rug.

"Goddamn it, all you motherfuckers, all you overeducated pricks. I cannot stand fucks like you, Cullen. And then what'd you do, hotshot? Sell out? Becoming somethin' even worse? A goddamn pig?"

Merle ignored Cullen's icy stare and hoisted the open, half-empty fifth of bourbon that stood on the floor by the couch. Socio-pathic psychotic that he was, he blithely changed the subject.

"Okay, this is what's going to go down. I'll be here tomorrow night at seven o'clock sharp. We're taking your car out there and waiting –"

"Waiting for what?"

"Our double date. Everything's been moved up. Other than that I ain't telling you shit." He was enjoying taunting Cullen, "I know you aren't going to pull anything funny. 'Cause you don't want Miss Goodie Two Shoes having any seven inch steel blade ventilatin' her titties. Am I right?"

Without warning, Cullen lashed out, flicking his cigarette in Merle's eyes, slamming him in the stomach then bringing his knee into the doubled-up man's face. Merle stumbled backwards into the wall, reached to draw his gun, but Cullen was on him before he could take aim and knocked it from his grasp. Both sets of their fists went flying, and within the next minute most of Cullen's living room was demolished. He was gaining the upper hand when suddenly dazed Merle, on the edge of unconsciousness, exploded upwards with a headbutt that sent Cullen onto the throwrug by the TV. Merle immediately grabbed the gun from the floor and squeezed off a shot that exploded the screen. He leveled the weapon at Cullen.

He muttered angrily through bloody, clenched teeth, "You're dyin' for me to make you eat shit, aren't you? Well, Cullen boy I'm up to it. Are you?"

"I was hoping you'd fire that and bring down some law."

Merle gave him a dripping crimson grin, "I doubt it. I made sure there was no one home on either side of you before dropping by. Just in case we had any differences of opinion. Good thing I was careful."

A beaten-to-a-pulp Cullen picked up the astonishingly-still-intact whiskey bottle and took a healthy swig. He glared at Merle. Merle reached out for it, "Gimme!"

Cullen just looked at him, then smashed the bottle at Merle's feet.

"I'll be here at seven tomorrow. Now get the fuck out."

Merle wiped his red mouth with his coatsleeve. "You bought yourself some time, lawman. That's all." He stumbled out, leaving Cullen alone in the ruins.

Mona stood at the bars of her cell, looking across the corridor at two women, one black, one white, having sex in the cell on the other side. The black woman leaned with her back against the bars, nuzzling the neck of her closed-eyed white lover. Then the white woman opened her eyes and gazed stoically at Mona. They locked stares, and Mona was unable to tear herself away.

A cricket started to sound, and Mona looked down. The grey insect chirped directly beneath her on the floor between her feet. Ignoring Debbie, who was obsessively reading a letter on the top bunk, Mona returned to her bed, sinking back onto the mattress with one arm behind her head.

Debbie's letter fluttered past, falling to the floor. Debbie slowly climbed down, out-of-character in her guard-down vulnerability. She walked to the metal mirror over the washbasin, reached out bracing herself with both hands on the sink and quietly wept.

Surprised, Mona watched her, then propped herself up and stretched to grab the letter. After a couple of seconds studying the paper, she looked back at Debbie. "Hey –" She reached out. "– Debbie."

Debbie yanked her arm away as Mona touched her. Mona would not give up, though, and tugged Debbie down to the bottom bunk. Debbie's protest was halfhearted,

"I don't want your pity."

Mona put her arms around Debbie's shoulders, and Debbie

started weeping again. Mona laid back against the wall, and Debbie nestled in the crook of her arm.

"I know Mom's dead now, but Manny didn't have to put Tina up for adoption –"

Terri and Tex strolled past other prisoners lounging both outside and inside their cells. Tex discreetly passed a piece of folded paper, obviously drugs, to Terri. Terri nodded. Tex's eyes went wide as they reached their cell.

Bettina's woman, Lucy, was rummaging through their stuff. She was crouched over Tex's bottom bunk with the mattress rolled back. Tex leapt on top of her, and a fight erupted.

When it started to look like Tex could really get hurt, Terri tried to separate them, but Lucy knocked her away. Debbie and other inmates congregated at the cell door, watching and cheering.

Mona could hear the chaos from down the corridor, but did not move, reading nonchalantly on her bed. Suddenly Bettina appeared in the open doorway, a malevolent smile on her demonic face.

"Above all the sex and violence, hunh?"

Mona put down her book and stared coldly at her visitor.

Bettina shrugged, "Me, too...hey, you got a smoke?"

Mona stayed stock still for a few seconds, then slowly stretched out to reach for a pack of cigarettes. Bettina lunged at her with a homemade toothbrush knife, and Mona tried to fold backwards, but ended up hitting the sink, and the blade barely grazed her side. Abruptly, the two were locked in a mortal struggle, banging into the bunk and finally toppling to the floor.

Down the corridor, Lucy had Tex in a headlock she couldn't escape. Tex tried to elbow her, to no avail. Terri jumped on Lucy's back, but Lucy slammed backwards into the wall, dislodging Terri. Suddenly guard Candice waded through the rowdy audience to break it up. She managed to free Tex, only to have Lucy turn her rage against her. Candice took up Tex's guitar and walloped Lucy with it. It cracked open, and twenty tiny paper dope packages spilled onto the floor. Tex was beside herself, no longer concerned about Lucy.

"Shit!"

She scrambled, crawling on all fours to scoop up the valuable packets. Terri watched with growing amazement.

Bettina almost connected to Mona's throat with her blade, but Mona clamped onto her wrist, spun her, then pivoted her up against the bars. With her other hand, she started banging Bettina's face into the metal rungs. Finally beaten, stupefied Bettina dropped the razor sharp toothbrush. She was nearly unconscious, and Mona had to prop her up as she reached down between her legs to retrieve the homemade shiv. She stuck it in Bettina's pants pocket, then tossed her out of the cubicle, kicking her in the ass so she banged against the opposite cell before slumping to the floor. Mona wearily shut her own barred door.

Back in Tex and Terri's cell, Lucy jumped Candice again, this time curling her powerful hands around her throat. Candice gasped for air, unable to break Lucy's grasp, and Terri lunged at Lucy, this time hitting her hard across the bridge of her nose.

Debbie was bitterly disappointed, "Terri, what-the-fuck you doing? That bitch needs to get hers."

Candice came loose just as more guards poured into the tiny cell. They immediately seized Lucy by both her arms and were about to do the same to Terri and Tex when Candice intervened, still massaging her throat.

"Those two are okay. Just Lucy." She fought to get her breath.

The other guards dragged the kicking, screaming hellcat, Lucy, out. More guards roughly shoved the crowd of convicts back to make way for them.

"All right, you bitches. Lockdown! You heard me. Back to your cells. Lockdown!

Candice stopped the procession as they came upon the groggy, prone Bettina.

Candice's croaking voice was down to a harsh whisper, but it was still full of poison, "What-the-fuck's your problem." She nudged Bettina's face with her foot and spotted the multiple bruises. She addressed one of the guards behind her.

"Pick up this piece of trash. Search her pockets."

The two guards continued past, squiring Lucy, who became even more agitated by the sight of the battered Bettina. She screamed in frustrated rage as she disappeared around the bend in the corridor. A guard hoisted Bettina up, propped her against the cell bars and immediately pulled out not only the knife but three packets of dope from the girl's jeans. Candice looked at Mona's cell.

Mona stood languidly, arms draped through her bars.

"What do you know about this?"

"She was high as hell stumbling down the hall and suddenly just passes out. Hit her head pretty hard. That's probably how her face got so black 'n' blue."

"Yeah...right." Candice gestured to the guard holding Bettina.

"Take her to solitary."

Candice turned back to look at Mona, absentmindedly rubbing her bruised throat. She slowly moved away, then she, too, was gone around the bend in the hall.

## 19

Cullen lay on the couch, bruised and battered, smoking a cigarette in the shadows. The window was open and the curtains drawn to reveal the full moon hanging in the lavender sky. He cocked his head to stare at it and let a thin stream of smoke out of his mouth, wafting into the ghostly light.

Merle had left the heater on full blast in his broiling trailer, something which made him toss all the more fitfully in his sleep.

He was in a dank, clanking cavern of stone and mortar illuminated by several oil lanterns. His father, a backwoods ogre of a man, worked maniacally, hovering over something obscured from Merle's vision. He repeatedly brought a large hammer down again and again, and Merle could hear the echoey, deafening bang of steel hitting steel, nails being pounded.

A whimpering cry issued from a small boy hunched against a clammy, wet wall.

His father casually looked over his shoulder at Merle. "Quit that cry baby shit, Merle. Or you'll get what your big brother's gettin'. At least he's takin' his punishment like a man."

Merle was suddenly up near the ceiling looking down. His elder 16-year-old brother was spread-eagled, nailed to the floor through his hands and feet by a monstrous parent.

Drenched from every pore, Merle exploded awake in terror, sat bolt upright and screamed.

Debbie leaned close against the wall and eavesdropped on the conversation between Terri and Tex in their cell.

"Now, Terri, you got to understand. This ain't dangerous at all. Do you think old Tex here would be involved otherwise? Your old man, Merle, set this up. At 9 PM tomorrow night we're going to be headed right over the wall."

"You are out of your fuckin' tree. No way am I tryin' anything like that. I'm totally chickenshit when it comes to the 'great escape' approach to doin' things."

Tex turned on her spigot of silky persuasion, "No, honey, you don't understand. There's no risk. Our old buddy, Candice, is paid off well and good to keep her nose out of this. So, it's an extra good thing you stepped in last night and saved her ass."

Terri gave her a doubtful look.

"Hey, what do you think about this? Mona's comin' too.

Terri rolled her eyes, "You must be crazy."

"No, no, no, Terri. Johnny Cullen, you know, the ex-cop? He's in on this with Merle."

"Now I know you're nuts. If there're two people who hate each other's guts, it's –"

"Okay, don't believe me. You see what I get from this place. And nobody's going to pull the wool over my eyes, baby doll, nobody. That's why I'm still in one piece."

"Oh, God."

"Stop your worryin'. It's worked out to a goddamn T."

They were quiet for a few moments, and Tex sucked on a cigarette.

Terri wanted to believe her. "It's real? All this escape shit? No pipe dream?" She reached over, pinched Tex's smoke and took a drag.

"Yeah, Terri. Yeah."

Terri was still reluctant, wary of how inept so many of the girls inside were and lamenting to herself just how little she really knew about Tex. Finally, she nodded. "All right."

"Good. I'm glad we're seein' eye to eye."

Debbie stepped into their cell. "It's all right by me, too. It's one of the most goddamn all right things I heard you lay down in a long time, Tex."

Tex was not happy. "What-the-fuck? You can't come."

"That ain't the way I see it."

"You bitch."

"I'm comin' with you or you're not goin' at all. You understand?"

"Why can't Debbie come, Tex? It seems like the more the merrier."

"I don't come, honey, you ain't goin' neither."

Tex paced to the bars as Mona entered. "Now look who's here. It's gettin' to be a regular goddamn slumber party."

Mona grimaced. "I heard most of it."

Tex just stared at Mona, then Debbie started to laugh. All four of them were clustered close together in the middle of the cell.

Mona shook her head, "The way you're broadcasting it, I'll be surprised if this whole place won't be ready at 9 PM tomorrow to go with us." She paused. "Personally, I can't wait to get the fuck out."

Terri was taken back by Mona's hardass demeanor, and Debbie laughed, "I guess that settles that."

Tex shrugged, "Okay, Debbie. I guess one extra monkey don't stop no show."

Harris and Springer were working together in their factory office, going over engineering plans on a drafting table.

"You figured out what we're doing about Chambers?"

Springer balked, "I don't know. You're the one who talked to Brantwell's man in L.A. What did he say?"

Harris smirked, "He said that the area out by Harbin's mining operation has countless old wells and sinkholes and abandoned mine shafts. That's what Brantwell's man in L.A. said."

There was the click of an opening and closing door, but neither turned around.

"Doris, I thought I told you we weren't to be disturbed."

There was the sound of a gun being cocked, then –

"Ain't that sweet."

Both of them whirled around, startled. Merle stood across the table, covering them with his .44.

"Two idealistic businessmen working together to build a better tomorrow."

Harris was more angry than scared, "What-the-fuck, Chambers?"

Laughing maniacally, Merle let loose, emptying his gun into the terrified men's bodies. They danced and writhed, finally slumping to the floor in geysers of blood.

Cullen's old Dodge Charger pulled away from the curb. Merle sprawled on the passenger seat, while Cullen drove.

"I don't guess I have to give you directions, do I?"

Cullen glanced at him, then returned his attention to the road. Merle stared at the side of Cullen's face as if he wanted to put a bullet through it.

Mona laid on her bunk, hands behind her head and stared at the ceiling. Debbie paced nervously. The lights had already gone out. Mona fired up a smoke, puffed, then handed it to Debbie. Debbie stopped abruptly.

"Thanks."

"Calm down. Everything's going to be okay. All that can happen is we get our brains blown out."

Debbie laughed, "Yeah, yeah. Now that you put it that way, it makes me feel a whole lot better."

A low whistle came from down the corridor, eerie and plaintive like one might hear on a lone prairie before a full-scale Indian attack.

Their cell door slid open. A chorus of whispers welled up from down the hall.

"Shit! Who'd Tex grease to get this goin'?"

"You mean who'd her old man grease!"

"Hey, looks like some bitches goin' out for an evenin' stroll."

"Stroll, my ass. Evenin' drag race. Right down the main drag of Dragsville."

Tex's voice rose up out of the chorus.

"Goddamn it, you two. C'mon if you're comin', elsewise –"
Before she could finish, Mona and Debbie slipped out into the corridor, making their way towards Tex and Terri. Tex peered through the tiny barred window of the hall door, ignoring the low catcalls from the cell block. She slowly rotated the knob, edging it open.

The prison buildings loomed in the distance behind the four running women. They arrived at the nine foot cement wall with electrified barb wire strung along the top.

"Somebody turnin' off the juice in those wires?" Debbie was overly anxious.

As if in answer, a wide rubber mat suddenly clunked down on top of and across the barb wire. No alarm sounded. A long chain descended over the mat from the other side.

Tex smiled. "My little buddy, Candice, sure knows how to take care of her friends. Terri, you first."

Terri looked at all of them with apprehension, then grabbed hold of the chain and started to hoist herself over. Tex jabbed Mona in the ribs.

"You next."

Mona followed suit without a word., but Tex was starting to get edgy. Mona disappeared over the wall.

Tex gazed at the barb wire and the rubber mat, suddenly nervous.

"Okay, Debbie."

Debbie spit in both palms, rubbed them together, then grabbed at the chain.

"Won't get no argument from me."

Halfway up, Tex made a move from beneath her denim jacket, and a long dagger of gleaming light flashed up into Debbie's guts. Debbie groaned and clutched her stomach as she fell.

"You cunt!" Her voice was hoarse and already hemorrhaging with bloody, wheezing breath.

"You asked for this, Debbie," Tex whispered angrily, "Couldn't leave well enough alone. Well, you made it, baby. All the fucking way!" Tex kicked her in the face, then scrambled quickly over the wall. Debbie turned over and tried to grab Tex's ankles, missed, then convulsed, vomiting blood. She died with a rattling gasp.

On the other side, Terri turned to see Tex coming down over the wall.

"Where's Merle?"

Tex came up to Mona and Terri who were standing next to a small tree where the chain end was tied. She pulled them along with her into a wooded area.

"Waiting in a car," She was trembling with impatience,

"He came up, fixed the mat and chain, then hightailed it so he wouldn't have to wait for us out in the open."

They continued through the trees. Realizing that Debbie was missing, Mona turned, walking backwards.

"I don't see Debbie."

"That's because she's not comin'. She turned yellow at the last minute."

Both Terri and Mona stopped and stared at each other.

"C'mon, you two, cut the shit!"

They stared at Tex.

"You cut the shit, Tex." Terri was hot with anger. "You know damn well Debbie isn't the kind to turn yellow at the last goddamn minute. Especially after pushing her way into this."

Tex was open-mouthed with amazement. Before she could answer, Mona piped in. "What'd you do, Tex? Pull the chain up before she could get hold? Or just stick a knife in her back?"

"Fuck you two! I ain't her keeper. You don't want to take my word, tough shit. But that's the way it happened. And we're gonna end up back there with her if we don't stop gabbin'."

She ran off ahead without them. Terri and Mona looked at each other, then followed.

They soon stumbled into a small clearing where Cullen's car was parked. Merle jumped out and gave Terri a kiss. "Hey, baby." Merle waved them to get in, not noticing Terri's wariness around him now.

"Tex, you drive. I'll sit on the other side with my buddy, Johnny Cullen, in the middle here – just so I can keep an eye on him."

Even though Mona knew he was coming, she was still shocked to see Cullen with Merle. They stared at each other, saying nothing. Cullen got back in.

Merle laughed, "Now we got his lil' girl safe and sound, I don't want him suddenly deciding to use his initiative. He's such an enterprising fellow."

Tex revved the car as Merle slid in next to Cullen from the passenger door. Terri climbed in the backseat, her gaze riveted on Mona who was still outside, rooted to the spot. Tex leaned over Cullen and Merle.

"Goddamn it. Get in the fuckin' car."

Terri glanced at Mona, then stared at the back of Merle's head.

"Don't worry, Mona. Nothing's going to happen to you and Johnny as long as I'm around."

Merle played the mock innocent. "What could happen to such a lovely, friendly couple?"

Mona continued to stare. Cullen reached over the seat and opened the other back door. Mona slowly slid in, her eyes never leaving Cullen. Tex gunned the engine, shot the car into drive, and they bolted down a dirt road with the headlights off.

Tex immediately began a tirade, "Goddamn it, Mona, what do you think this is? A goddamn fashion show? Or maybe one of those kindergarten classes you used to teach? I can't tell you how sick I am of your uppity bullshit."

Merle casually looked over at Tex, "Knock off the tantrums and pay attention to the road."

Tex glared at him, but shut up. Merle popped a cassette into the car stereo and a hard as nails speed metal anthem blared in the enclosed space. Cullen reached over to cut the volume in half. Merle gave him a stare but said nothing.

They drove for at least half an hour without further interruption.

## 20

Mist clung to the black trees as they plummeted down a rural asphalt road in the darkness. Tex finally turned the headlights on. She switched on the wipers to cut the accumulating drizzle and strained over the wheel to see the stretch of road immediately ahead of them. Merle pointed, "There's a turn here in about half a mile."

Suddenly Cullen grabbed Merle's gun hand, forcing it up against the ceiling. A shot rang out, nearly deafening them all. Merle dropped the gun between Tex's legs as the two struggled.

"Stop it, you assholes, I can't drive like this!"

Mona and Terri were frozen with fear and strangely silent as the fighting continued. Then Mona came alive, pulling back on Merle's head. Tex reached down, picked up the gun with her left hand and fired it nearly point blank into Cullen's left arm.

Almost simultaneously there was a screeching as the car swerved. Tex tried to regain control but it was too late. There was an audible, sickening wrenching of metal as she slammed on the brakes. And then came the crash. It turned over, sliding on its side, then slipped off of the road. When it at last came to rest, there was virtually no sound except the settling crunch of twisted metal. A chorus of moans and groans gradually welled up from inside.

The windshield was broken. Tex's bloody head rested on the crumpled dash. Mona and Terri were scratched up, but they scrambled out largely unhurt. Mona helped the wounded Cullen climb free while Merle pulled Tex's limp form through the windshield and onto the roadside.

Merle had a gash across his cheek but was oblivious as he listened at Tex's chest. Terri knelt and felt her pulse.

Merle straightened up. "I don't believe this." He bent down again, shaking Tex, then once more listened for a heartbeat.

"Goddamn it to fucking hell!" He looked at Terri. "Andy told her where we should head to lay low. Stuff I don't know." Abruptly, he was on his feet, lunging towards Cullen and knocking him down. "This is your goddamn fault, you cocksucker!"

Terri reached Merle, pulling him back as Mona helped Cullen to stand.

"I really ought to fucking waste your ass right fucking now."

Merle broke away from Terri, ran back to the car, burying his top half inside the broken windshield. It took only a few seconds, and he reemerged with the gun. He careened towards Cullen and Mona, pointing it.

"I should do you *both*."

Terri latched onto his gun hand. "What-the-fuck are you talking about, Merle?"

Merle looked at her as she jerked his hand away. He wheeled back towards the car, stared up into the sky with raised arms and roared out a bloodcurdling scream.

It seemed to calm him down. "All right, this ain't gonna slow us up." He motioned with the gun. "Let's get crackin'. We walk."

Mona and Cullen started stumbling along the road.

Merle shout-whispered "In the trees, you dimwits." He lagged a few paces behind, driving them on. Terri drifted back to be with him, and Mona and Cullen took the lead. As they made their way through the woods, Mona tore a piece of her denim shirt sleeve as a bandage and wrapped it around Cullen's upper arm.

"You are so damn lucky it didn't hit an artery. Especially point blank like that."

Cullen whispered. "It's only a matter of time before I get the gun away from him."

"You're as crazy as he is."

Cullen kept his voice low.

"The son-of-a-bitch'll give out eventually. He's got guts, but when it comes to endurance, he's a big baby. And he is going to kill us eventually, unless we do him first."

"Maybe. Only thing, Johnny, I'm not leaving Terri with him, no matter what happens."

Growing paranoid, Merle closed ground, "Hey, you two, keep your traps shut."

They trudged on in silence.

Night in the forest was lit by shadowy moonlight. Cullen and Mona slept in each others' arms beneath a redwood tree. Merle and Terri lay a few yards closer to the road, still awake. Merle sat up, studying Cullen and Mona.

Terri was anxious about Merle's state of mind. "What?"

"What do you mean 'what'?"

"What're you lookin' at them for?"

"I want to make sure they're asleep, stupid."

Terri propped herself on one elbow, getting mad. Merle stood, dusted off the leaves and dirt, then gingerly moved away.

"Where-the-fuck do you think you're goin'?"

Merle skulked back to her in a crouching walk, angrily whispering, "To get us a car. Now shut your piehole before you wake those two."

"How the hell are you going to get us a car way out here?"

"Shut the fuck up, Terri. I'm not tellin' you again. And if I come back and you've made a sound, or those two are gone, I'm going to beat the living daylights out of you."

She stared at him with angry eyes as he slunk off into the trees.

The gas station was closed, with one lone blue light shining from the office. Merle crouched behind some bushes, just a few feet from a lonely pay telephone booth alongside the deserted mountain highway. He shivered and winced, surveying his surroundings apprehensively, then lighting a cigarette. Time was like defrosting molasses.

Headlights appeared out of the darkness. Merle took a final drag and ground out the smoke. A Highway Patrol car whizzed past, and he frowned. Almost immediately, the sound of another car welled up in the distance. Lights blinded Merle as a station wagon driven by a couple in their mid-thirties pulled over next to the phone.

Merle moved stealthily closer.

The woman driver emerged from the car and walked to the booth. Merle was suddenly standing next to her, covering her with his gun. He didn't say anything, instead motioning the woman around to the passenger side of the car. The man inside was listening to the radio. When the car door opened, he still hadn't noticed Merle.

"What's the matter? No chan –" He stopped mid-word as he spotted Merle over his wife's shoulder.

Merle gestured with the huge gun, "Get out."

The man glanced in the back of the car, then up at his wife who was starting to cry.

"But – but –"

Merle reached around the woman, slapping the man in the head with the gun muzzle. The man recoiled, then slowly straightened again with a gushing crimson gash on his temple. His trembling, terrified wife helped him out of the car.

Merle impatiently wagged the .44, "C'mon, goddamn it."

They preceded Merle into the woods. He finally stopped them in a small comparatively open space.

"This is it." He held out his free left hand, "Gimme your jacket, buddy."

The nearly hysterical woman's gaze darted frantically back and forth between the two men as her husband nervously stripped off his bloodstained brown corduroy jacket. Merle hurriedly grabbed it, wrapping it around the muzzle of his gun. The couple huddled together, holding onto each other.

"No – NO – NOOO – !" Merle quickly shot both of them in the head to cut off her rising-to-a-scream voice.

He didn't even give their corpses a second glance before he was traipsing back to the station wagon. He jumped in, started the car and drove off, relieved at finding the car and totally free from any remorse.

"Mommy, Mommy –" The voice of a small child from the back seat made Merle jump.

He adjusted the rearview mirror, and his eyes went wide with shocked surprise. There was the screeching of brakes. He ricocheted around to stare at a very young boy sitting in the back seat, then whipped his head back round to stare out the windshield. The little boy was the spitting image of himself at that age. Merle tightly clutched at the steering wheel. A wide-ranging gamut of conflicting emotions ran over his suddenly sweat-drenched features.

"Hey, where's Mommy and Daddy?"

Merle did not answer as he suddenly put one arm on the back of the seat, looking backwards as he drove in reverse, returning to the gas station that was a few hundred meters away. He braked, jumped out of the car, threw open the back door, scooped the youngster out and carried him to the phone booth. The little boy started to cry.

Merle set him down inside, stooping to look into the kid's face.

"Stop your yammering. Your Mommy and Daddy will be back real soon. You need to stay here and wait for 'em."

The boy sniffled, trying to be brave but Merle obviously scared-the-hell out of him.

Merle hurriedly stood again and, without a backward glance, raced to the car, leapt in and careened off. He went about a sixth of a mile, speeding down the highway, before throwing on the brakes again. Once more there was a terrible screeching, a noise that made Merle feel as if his insides were being clawed out.

He stared into the rearview mirror. Without warning, Merle started screaming, hitting at the car ceiling, the windshield, the dash, anything in reach with his already bruised fists. Just as quickly, he became totally stoic, placed one arm again on the seat back as his eyes fixed on the telephone booth target at the gas station. He accelerated in reverse at a terrifying speed, heading straight for it. Just before he hit it, he screamed again, his voice an anguished cry from the depths of Hell.

The telephone booth obliterated, another witness no longer a danger to him, Merle threw the car violently into drive and roared away in a cloud of dust.

Mona tossed fitfully. Cullen turned on his right side, with his back to her, half-asleep, trying to get comfortable with his damaged left arm.

A glowing blue mist crept between the trees.

Mona sleepily opened her eyes.

Rose Martin, clad in a simple white dress, appeared before her from the shadows. She put an index finger to her lips, motioning to keep quiet, then beckoned. Mona glanced at Cullen, then slowly rose up, following Rose into the trees. There was the sound of familiar voices just beyond. Right after the next tree her mother, Consuela, and her father, Pete, sitting on a fallen tree, came into view.

They both held sparklers and were laughing.

"Papa! Mama!"

They looked over at the sound of her voice and became silent.

"Who are you?" her mother asked.

Mona was crestfallen.

"What did you call us?" asked her father. Puzzled, he turned to look at Consuela, "The girl's crazy."

Rose took hold of Mona and led her away. She put an arm around Mona's shoulders in a protective, affectionate gesture, and they plunged deeper into the forest.

"It's okay, Mona. They don't recognize anyone since they got back together."

Mona stopped in her tracks, flabbergasted.

"Rose, you can talk."

Rose smiled, "Of course, I can talk. Come on, there are people waiting to see you." The bluish mist was replaced by alternately lavender and yellow glowing patches. They came into a large clearing. Merle sat eating chicken atop the rusty gutted shell of Cullen's Dodge Charger. A raven cawed from its perch on the open door. A huge campfire blazed on the ground next to the ruined chassis. Another fat chicken roasted above it on a makeshift spit. Merle grinned down on them as Rose led Mona past the fire. He jumped to their side good-naturedly, embracing Mona and kissing her on the cheek. Mona was dumbfounded.

"It's good to see you, Mona. I didn't think you'd ever make it."

"Where's Terri?"

"Taking a nap somewhere."

Rose pulled Mona from his grasp, steering her toward the other side of the car. Four prone bodies covered by sheets lay in the mud. Smiling Rose yanked off the first sheet, and Mona gasped as her mother, Consuela, came into view. Rose took off the next two sheets simultaneously, and Cullen and Terri's bloody bodies were revealed. Mona kneeled down beside the last covered corpse. Rose joined her, kissed her on the cheek as Mona pulled aside the last sheet to reveal herself. Her eyes went wide. Merle roughly grabbed hold of her, gripping her forehead steady with his left hand then drawing a large butcher knife across her jugular, slitting her throat.

Mona jumped from sleep with a crazy yell. Immediately, Cullen was sitting up beside her, arms around her, soothing her. Terri crawled over.

"What's the matter?"

"Just a bad dream." Cullen explained. Mona was spaced-out. Terri and Cullen gently lay her back down.

"She'll be okay."

Terri nodded, frowning. Distracted, she got to her feet and wandered into the trees. Cullen straightened horizontal beside Mona, wincing at his damaged shoulder.

Terri leaned against a redwood, pulled out a pack of smokes and lit one. She heard the noise of twigs snapping, and she discarded the cigarette, grinding it out. She moved cautiously forward. A few yards further on she stopped and watched.

The stolen station wagon was parked between two trees in a shallow glen. Merle was crouched behind it, smearing mud over the rear license plate. Terri walked up to him. He stopped for a second, glancing in her direction, then continued with his task.

"Wow, you got a car."

He didn't say anything.

"What're you doing?"

"What does it look like?"

She didn't reply, instead opening the front passenger door and playfully bouncing down onto the seat. Reflexively, she yanked her hand away from something sticky on the fake leather upholstery. She reached over with her other hand to turn on the dome light. Her palm was smeared with blood. She lurched around to the back seat and saw a child's blanket and a toy rubber duckie on the vinyl covering. She rushed over behind the car to the crouching Merle and stretched out her bloody hand to him.

"What-the-fuck is this?"

Merle ignored her.

"Goddamn it, Merle. Answer me."

"What do you want me to say? It's your hand."

"What about the blood?"

"I cut myself."

"Bullshit."

"Fuck you if you don't believe me."

"Did – did you kill someone to get this thing?"

"Nah. Of course not. You know me better than that."

Terri backed away, "I don't believe you."

"We got a car. Now shut up!"

She backed further away, "I'm not standing for this shit."

Merle lunged forward, flattening himself on the ground as he clawed after Terri. He caught her around one ankle and pulled her back down the gentle slope. She hit him around the head and shoulders with her fists, and he yanked her beneath him, putting one hand over her mouth.

"Goddamn you, Terri. Shut up. Who gives a fuck about some suburban whore, her pathetic hubby and their bastard kid?"

Terri bit his hand, "Merle, you asshole. You ain't got any corner on the god market. You? YOU? Judge and jury for some poor –"

"Shut up, Terri! I mean it!" He tightened his palm around her throat. "We got a car now. And if you don't shut your mouth, I'll shut it for you."

Terri stared at him, afraid, but still belligerent.

"Okay, okay. I'll shut up. I just don't understand why-the-hell you bothered to break us out of the joint in the first place."

She slowly crawled out from under him.

Merle grew patronizing. "Because I missed you, baby. You know you're the closest thing I got to kin. Besides, I wanted to have some fun with Mr. Johnny Cullen. Him and your halfbreed sis. I got plans for both of them on my lil' ole agenda."

His eyes followed her as she regained her feet and stumbled away.

## 21

Terri crouched beside Mona, then curled up against her other side, shivering all the while. It was finally dawning on her how much the drugs had really blinded her, just how crazy Merle really was, and it scared her from the tingling roots of her hair down to the tips of her chafed toes.

There was the sound of crunching dead leaves under a heavy tread. A pair of dirty shoes came into view. Terri looked up to see Merle nonchalantly smoking, staring down at her. He walked away into the shadows without saying a word.

The barely risen sun peeked through a myriad set of branches. Cullen's open eyes gleamed in the shadows. Mona stirred, hugged him tighter and sleepily opened her eyes.

They immediately surrendered to a sexual hunger, kissing lustily and were near to shedding their clothes if not for the proximity of unwanted company. Reluctantly, they let their passion subside. Mona lay her head on Cullen's shoulder. They rested together in peace for an all too few minutes. She barely touched his wounded arm.

"How is that? It isn't still bleeding, is it?"

Cullen shook his head distractedly. He was pale from the loss of blood, but he was not disturbed by this. However, there was something preying on his mind.

"I had a nightmare last night, too. It was the same dream I had when I first came over to your house, the night your mother died."

Mona turned her face to look up at him.

"I don't remember much. We were together like we are now running from something. We knew we wouldn't be together for very long. I didn't understand what it was all about then."

"We *are* going to be together." She was unsure of herself. "You know the nightmare I had? Everyone was dead. All of us anyway. And Merle was the only one left alive."

Terri, still lying concealed next to Mona, sat bolt upright, staring at them with horror, and they noticed her for the first time. No one spoke. Terri slowly rose up, backing away from them, then started running. Before she'd gotten more than twenty yards, Merle popped out from behind a tree and threw her to the ground.

"What's the matter, baby?"

She couldn't answer.

"Cat got your tongue, sugar buns? Well, c'mon and get your skinny ass in gear. We're clearing out – now."

The station wagon swerved, climbing a steep incline on the mountain. Terri drove, with Mona sitting in front beside her. Cullen was in the back next to a restless Merle, who was fidgeting with the gun in his lap. Merle looked around and noticed something in the very back of the car.

"Hey, look what we got here." He pivoted to the front, displaying a boom box in his left hand and placing it on the seat. Curiosity getting the better of her, Terri glanced in the rearview mirror. She risked swiveling her head to take a look before returning her attention to the road. Merle pushed the play button, and an insipid children's song blasted from the speakers. It unnerved Terri, and she swerved slightly. Merle ejected the cassette and tossed it out the window.

"Hey, baby, drive in a straight line, would you? As a special favor to me."

Mona glanced back at him disgustedly. Unfortunately, everything he was doing with the boom box was with his left hand,

and he still had hold of the gun.

"You know what I've got in my pocket, Terri?" He rummaged in his jeans, and gave Cullen a dirty look. "Although we never got a chance to play it in Detective Cullen's bucket of bolts." He pulled the cassette out, "Your favorite tape." He inserted it into the boom box and cranked up the volume.

It was Terri's former band.

"Christ, Merle." She was not happy hearing it. "Do you have to? It's so fuckin' painful to listen to."

"Why? You mean 'cause you guys didn't exactly light fires under any record company executives' asses?"

"How were we supposed to, playing only one gig in L.A.?"

"Yeah, you're right. Tough break. Nobody was knockin' down your door to get you to sign on the dotted line. No shooting stars in the – what would you call it? – celestial firmament?"

Mona leaned over the back of the seat. "Give it a rest."

Merle looked at her as if he wanted to rip her larynx out. Terri nervously asked, "Merle, can you turn it down a little?"

Mona wouldn't let it lie. "Better yet, how about give us all a break. You know she doesn't want to listen to it. Turn it off."

Surprised, Merle was unsure how to react. Feeling unsure of himself, he did a double take on Cullen, who was also giving him the evil eye. Abruptly he threw the whole contraption out the window, and it clattered and banged on the asphalt as it quickly disappeared in the distance.

Mona wanted to rub it in, "Is that a good idea, Merle? Aren't you the big mastermind? They might find your prints all over that ghetto blaster."

Merle gave out with a corrosive laugh.

Cullen changed the subject, "So Merle, where you got us headed? There'll be roadblocks thrown up along here anytime now."

"We've only got a couple more miles, then we're headed up a dirt road to a lil' mountain cabin I know of. Real nice. Might as well be invisible. From the air, it looks like it's covered by trees." He paused, "But we do have to stop and pick up some supplies. There'll be a store comin' up here before too long. It goes without saying, Johnny boy here's going to stick in people's minds what with the hole in his arm. And they don't get too many uppity bitches like Mona chilling out in this neck of the woods. So, Terri, I guess you're elected to do the grocery shopping"

They pulled up in front of a small mountain store. An elderly couple exited from the dingy establishment.

Merle handed Terri a wad of cash. She started to get out, but Merle grabbed onto one arm. He adopted a condescending tone, "Honey, it might be a good idea to put on your jacket, cover up all those tattoos." Tugging herself away from him, Terri slipped into her denim jacket, then piled out.

Terri climbed the few rickety steps to the entrance.

As Terri paid for the groceries, the store clerk glanced at a newspaper he had on the shelf beneath the cash register. Three large shots of Terri, Mona and Tex were spread across the front page and below them, smaller photos of Cullen and Merle. Terri, zombie-like, trudged out with the groceries, oblivious to the clerk's rapt interest.

Billie Travers sat behind her desk, a toothpick in her mouth and feet propped up. She thumbed through a newspaper, amused at the day's events. Jerry was in uniform but sported an incongruous baseball cap.

"You think Cullen's with 'em, Billie?

Billie grimaced at Jerry's stupidity, "I'd stake my reputation on it."

"State troopers going to let you in on this?"

"Damn straight. And when I find that bunch, I'm going to bust John Cullen's candy ass from here to kingdom come."

The phone rang, and Travers pounced on it.

"Yeah, it's me – Unh, hunh – I see. Thanks for the tip, Jeff."

She hung up the phone, stood, then looked out the window.

"They've been sighted, Jerry. Up about 20 miles, way past Santa Mira at a little country store. Get your ass in gear."

She took the toothpick out of her mouth and broke it in two.

The station wagon hurtled up the mountain road.

Mona leaned over to Terri, "We should never have listened to Tex. We're going to be caught anytime now. All this will wipe out any chance of parole."

Merle snorted with laughter. "You are too much."

Terri was resigned to their fate, "Honey, I'd rather they kill me than have to go back to that zoo."

Mona was surprised by Terri's remark.

Merle chimed in, "Plus you guys'll get blamed for murdering Debbie, along with dead Tex."

Mona swiveled around, "What are you talking about?'

"I know you already guessed it."

Terri was shaken, "We were giving Tex shit because she was being such a bitch."

"Tex was a hard ass. She and I saw eye-to-eye on a lot of things. Snuffing some loose cannon cunt like Debbie who muscled her way into where she didn't belong, we're on the same wavelength on shit like that. She told me when she got to the car with you two. Just 'cause she didn't shout it from the rooftops, so you three squares could hear, doesn't mean it ain't so."

Terri was livid. "Scumbag."

Merle laughed again.

"I'm talkin' about the *both* of you, Merle."

Merle stopped laughing and looked at Terri as if he was going to strangle her, whether it caused them to run off the steep mountain road or not.

Cullen turned to face front after looking at the patch of highway they had left behind.

"See anything?" Mona asked.

"No. I can't believe we haven't run into any roadblocks yet."

Merle's demeanor boomeranged, and he continued laughing, "How many times do I have to tell you? Where we're headed is comin' up any minute now." Merle got excited, pointing.

"There she is, Terri. Turn. Goddamn it, turn here."

Confused, Terri jerked the car to the left across the road, almost rolling it.

Merle lost his temper, "Watch it, goddamn it."

They went spiraling up a wide unpaved road. After a minute or so, the forest fell away, leaving a large clearing. A small shack was tucked up underneath the trees at the opposite end.

Mona groaned, "Oh, Christ!"

Terri was disgusted, "You're nuts, Merle."

"What did you expect? The Hilton?"

They rolled to a stop beside the shack, but Merle shook his head.

"No, no, no. Around the back. Pull into the woods. Nobody'll ever see the car from the road. Or the air."

Terri gingerly steered the car around the shabby hut, then under a big clump of overhanging trees. Branches obscured vision, brushing across the windshield. Merle reached over, switched off the ignition, then pocketed the keys.

"Everybody out."

Mona turned to look at Cullen. Merle held the door open. "Out, I said."

Cullen disembarked, and Mona and Teri followed. As he jumped out himself, Merle kept a wary eye on Cullen and kept him covered. He then flipped open the engine hood, removed the distributor cap, unscrewed the coil and pocketed it.

"Just so there's no misunderstandings later."

All at once, there was the whoosh-whoosh of a helicopter approaching.

"Shit!" He gestured at the shack, "In through that door. Quick!"

Mona and Cullen's attention was directed at the copter above.

"You two are looking kind of hopeful. Well, don't be. You two kill me. You should be workin' with me to stay away from them. I don't know what-the-fuck you think they're gonna do to you when they catch up with you. You're in the same fix as I am."

Mona and Cullen didn't say anything and walked into the dark shack.

Terri kicked at the ramshackle wall and wrecked furniture. "You're the one who kills me, Merle. Look at this joint. No electricity, no plumbing, no nothin'. And we're cut off from everything."

"That's the general idea. It's not as cool as what Tex and Andy had in mind, but –" he reached behind the ashen black oil stove and came up with another boom box. He tossed it to Terri. "Catch!" She barely snagged it before it hit the ground.

The chopper faded into the distance. Everyone was quiet.

"Why didn't you try to call Andy last night?" Terri wanted to know, "Find out what they'd set up?"

Merle was disgusted with her naiveté, "Because once Andy finds out Tex is dead we couldn't trust him as far as we could throw him."

Suddenly, Merle reached out and latched onto Mona's arm.

"C'mon, you're going with me."

She tried to resist. Cullen moved towards them, but Merle waved him away with the gun, amused at Cullen's chivalry. "You're funny, lawman. I'm not doin' nothin' freaky with your bitch. Just takin' her with me while I run a little errand in the hills. Get some more much needed supplies. Just so you'll be here when I get back. I ain't gonna touch a hair on her prissy little head. Not unless she gets funny with me."

Mona put up her hand to ward off Cullen. "It's okay, Johnny, I'll be all right."

Merle laughed. "That's right – Johnny. Listen to your old lady."

They left.

Terri turned to Cullen, watching him as he painfully sat himself down on the littered floor.

"I know what you're thinkin'. When the right time comes, you're going to kill him. I can't say I haven't entertained the notion myself. Especially after last night. He killed to get that car. He's been killing right along."

"Don't tell me that's news to you?"

Terri became defensive, "I don't believe he killed Mama. I just can't."

"You're in denial. You know now she was murdered. Forensics proved it. Who else was there with Consuela before you and Mona got home? He was the only one."

Terri's head felt as if it was going to explode, and she pressed her hands to her temples to try to keep it from happening, "The one thing he's got goin' for him is he really knows this hustle. He's got nothin' to lose. He's a monster. That's why I think he might get us out of this alive."

"You, maybe. Not me and Mona. He'd rather die himself than let the two of us live."

Mona and Merle were out in the open stumbling over a hilly land-scape dotted with weeds and a few scattered trees and shrubs. Merle continually watched the heavens with a paranoid eye. Mona was resigned to her fate and was slowly beginning to look at her situation with detached amusement.

They approached a small squat shed that resembled an outhouse. Merle scrambled to it, plugged a key into the padlock, then ripped open the door. Mona squinted to see what was inside. Merle grabbed two large dusty knapsacks and started loading the contents of the lean-to into it: numerous sticks of dynamite. Once the two sacks were nearly full, he picked up a cigar box full of primers, a rusty plunger and roll of cable wire, jamming them all carefully into the overflowing bags. Lastly, he slung a high-powered rifle with a telescopic sight over his shoulder. He pocketed a box of ammunition in his jacket pocket.

Mona smiled wryly, "I guess this is your contingency plan."

Merle was proud of himself, "My big brother used to call me a one-man army. That was before Pa nailed him to the floor down in Houston."

He cinched up the knapsacks' cords as if they were around someone's neck. Mona tensed at his erratic behavior.

Merle's voice became strange and dreamy, "Pa...Fuckin' Pa! He really did nail Dez to the floor when Ma was out. Crucified him, the drunken son-of-a-bitch. A few nights later, Mama stuck a sawed-off shotgun in his mouth while he was asleep –"

Abruptly, he remembered himself. He came up close to her as she lit a cigarette, and he calmly put a hand on one of her breasts. Mona brought a stick of dynamite up between them, holding the fuse only centimeters away from the glowing tobacco embers.

Beads of sweat broke out on Merle's forehead, and he gulped, swallowing uneasily, "It's really too bad Bettina fucked things up. It would've made things alot easier not having you along."

"Then again, Terri might not have come. That was your 'reasoning', right?"

He very carefully removed his hand from her chest as he backed away. "Yeah, but it still would have been nice if Bettina had gotten her shit together."

"Why doesn't it surprise me you had something to do with that?"

Merle stopped to pick up the sacks and handed one to Mona. "Actually it was Travers put the contract out on you."

Mona was shocked.

"Shit, girl, she's got a hell of a lot more reason to hate your guts than me. You – you took her goddamn man."

Mona just stared at him.

Merle slowly reached up to her face, removed the smoke from between her lips, then dropped it and ground it out under his heel. He slung a bandolier of ammunition around her neck.

"C'mon, you holier-than-thou bitch. Your boyfriend's going to start knittin' his brow.

Cullen was perched on the back step, watching for a sign of the two's return. He spotted Mona and Merle cresting one of the hills as at last they came into view. When Mona and Merle finally reached the back door, Merle roughly snatched the bandolier from around Mona's head and her knapsack, then continued inside. But Mona stood still, staring at Cullen.

Inside, Merle rummaged in the sacks. He finally found what he wanted, a small slender leather case, and he opened it, taking out a syringe, a bent spoon, a tiny bottle of water and some dope. Terri watched him without emotion. He sat crosslegged on the floor and leaned against the wall, facing the screen door with the rifle between his legs and preparing his shot of heroin.

Merle didn't look up, transfixed by the ritual at hand, "You want a taste, too, am I right?

Terri uncomfortably hesitated. "No... I think I'm going to pass."

Twenty minutes later, Terri stared down at a nodded-out Merle, slumped over his rifle. The thought of blowing his brains out crossed quickly through her mind. But she knew she couldn't do it. She kicked the paraphernalia across the room, then went restlessly to the back screen door and stared outside. Where were Mona and Cullen? She couldn't see them. She smacked the door open and stepped outside to look around. The dry leaves crackled under her feet. She heard a noise from the station wagon.

Cullen was lying on his back with his shirt off on the rear seat. Mona was on top of him, also naked from the waist up, her full breasts pressed against his chest and her hair falling down around him, almost obscuring his face. Blackened, almost dried blood from Cullen's bullet wound mingled with both their sweat. Their wild, open-mouthed kiss and partial nudity embarrassed Terri.

There was a pain inside her she found horribly confusing – part envy wanting what they had, jealousy that they had it while her seemingly uninhibited, intimate relationship with Merle was really anything but; part anger at herself that she had willfully turned a blind

eye to how barren her life was; part hatred of herself that she had let
Merle pull her into his freakish, elliptical orbit.

She watched the two of them as they stripped off each others'
pants and coupled on the back seat in the car of the poor dead family
Merle had murdered. She was glad for Mona. Funny – now was the
perfect time for the two to get the better of Merle while he was on the
nod. But they were too busy fucking. The complex rush of emotions
made her gorge rise, and she suddenly found herself on her knees,
vomiting in the dirt.

## 22

Merle was busily trying to finish mining the point where the dirt road spilled into the clearing, the area directly opposite from the partially hidden shack. He covered over a shallow, 20 foot long trench filled with dynamite. Emerging from the soil, yards and yards of detonating wire trailed back up to the cabin.

Terri warily approached.

"What're you gonna do, Merle? Blow up the whole damn world?"

He rubbed his dusty bare chest but didn't look at her, "If I have to."

"And anybody who stands in your way?"

"That goes without saying." He shielded his eyes from the sun as he smiled up at her. "You already knew the answer to that, baby."

"Blow me up, too?"

Merle nodded as he casually lit up a cigarette.

"You don't give me much reason to stick around."

He touched the gun in his belt, "You got plenty of reason."

"You wouldn't fucking dare."

Merle laughed, "Yeah?"

He exhaled a toxic lungful of smoke, "Hey, if I didn't let your sickass, bitch stepmother get away with anything, what makes you think you'll be any different?"

Terri was livid, eyes widening.

"You bastard. You did kill her."

Merle just laughed. Terri jumped on his back, her claws out. Merle yelled and reached for his gun, but Terri frantically knocked it from his grasp. They rolled over on the ground, fighting furiously tooth and nail, and came to rest against some shrubs.

Cullen heard the commotion and rushed down the slight incline to their side. He tried to pull Terri from Merle, simultaneously giving Merle a hard right cross to the jaw to facilitate the process. Terri lashed back instinctively, elbowing Cullen in the face. Cullen grabbed out for her again, and got her off him. Bruised and bleeding, amused Merle lay beside some desiccated shrubs, smiling a bloody smile, hands behind his head in an attitude of mock relaxation. Cullen was at a disadvantage with only one good arm. Terri broke loose again, and Merle laughed. She glared at him with abject hatred, spotted a large stone on the ground and, in one continuous lightning motion, picked it up with both hands and brought it down on his startled face, killing him.

Blood gurgled and streamed from Merle's open mouth, from his nose and his battered eyes.

Cullen stumbled awkwardly to his feet, incredulous at the death scene. Mona approached from behind him, her hands going up to her mouth when she spotted Merle.

Terri stood there in shock. She slowly sat down cross-legged on the ground, her eyes fixed on her dead lover.

Cullen held onto his now-bleeding arm, "Well, it looks as if you've solved one problem."

The dusk deepened and night fell.

As the sun rose the next morning, Terri slit open and fixed the wire cable leading from the dynamite to the plunger detonator that sat in the center of the shack's littered floor.

Terri glanced over at Mona. "This is about the only thing Merle ever taught me."

Mona and Cullen looked at each other with hopeless expressions. Mona turned to gaze out the window. Cullen rose, grabbing the spade propped against the wall by the back door and left. He casually walked around the edge of the clearing, staying close to the trees and watching the skies. He made his way to Merle's body, set down the shovel, then with one arm painfully dragged Merle behind the bushes. Wearily, he started to dig Merle's grave.

Mona was suddenly standing next to him. She pulled the shovel from his grasp and began to dig herself.

Terri pressed a button and set the ghetto blaster roaring an old school punk rock song from the late seventies. She walked over to one of the dynamite sacks and withdrew more dynamite, then grabbed the rifle and bandolier. She pulled out cartridges and began loading the rifle.

Mona and Cullen were tamping down the dirt on Merle's grave and turned at the sound of the loud music.

Cullen frowned. "They can probably here that for miles."

Mona turned to him, "We're not going to get out of here, are we?"

Cullen hesitated and shook his head, "By now I'm sure they know I'm involved in all this."

Mona suddenly kissed him passionately on the mouth. "Thanks for everything you've tried to do, John. Maybe if you could just take off now, maybe they'd never know – " Mona pulled the distributor coil out of her denim jacket pocket, "Merle threw away the keys, but you could hotwire –"

His look stopped her cold. "I'm not going anywhere, Mona. Even if I could. I can't."

Travers's voice startled them both, "That's right, John, you can't."

Mona and Cullen stood stock still as Billie Travers appeared from behind a tree and some dry brown shrubbery, a drawn revolver in her hand. She motioned, and Jerry came out of the underbrush with two other deputies Cullen didn't recognize.

A cop on a motorcycle, a sheriff's cruiser and two state police cars pulled up to where the dirt road spilled into the clearing, blocking any escape. Travers obsessively locked her gaze on Mona.

"Who's left in the cabin, John?"

Cullen and Mona stared at each other. Travers turned slightly to glare at Cullen. Her voice was calm, but nastily vindictive. "You don't want to talk, John? You didn't always used to be on such a high horse. Not until this piece of –" She cut herself short. "Suddenly you got sophisticated, sensitive, better than everybody else."

Cullen ignored her.

"C'mon, John, it's no use. We know Chambers is dead. We saw you two bury him. Thank God for small favors. Now who's still up there? The Highway Patrol found Tex and the car. Who is it? Terri?"

The crack of rifle shots came as an answer. The motorcycle cop and one of the other deputies fell dead. Travers and the other lawmen flattened on the ground.

Travers looked up at Cullen and Mona, "Get down here! Do you think she gives a damn at this point who she kills?"

Cullen slowly crouched. Mona followed suit, staring fixedly at the shack.

Travers motioned to Jerry. "Give me that bullhorn!" Jerry held it out, and she grabbed it.

Travers addressed her officers, "Okay, men, hold your fire until I say so –" then she shouted into the bullhorn, "Hey, you in the cabin. Terri? We got Mona and Cullen. Come on out with your arms raised over your head."

More rifle shots came in answer.

Travers glowered at Mona, "Doesn't give a damn, does she? That is who's up there, right? Just Terri?"

Mona couldn't answer.

Cullen spoke up. "It's just her sister, Terri."

Without warning, Mona panicked and tried to run to the shack. Cullen and Travers caught her by the ankles and yanked her down. Travers called into the bullhorn, "Terri, stop it. C'mon out and give yourself up."

Terri crawled on all fours across the floor. She edged up to the front window.

"Fuck you all! I'm never going back!"

She let loose with another barrage of shots.

Travers shouted, "Okay, men, open fire."

Mona screamed, "No, Terri!"

Cullen was having trouble keeping Mona down, what with his bad arm.

Terri's shouting from the shack was barely audible above the gunfire. "Mona, get-the-fuck away from here. I'm gonna die here... There's no other way out!"

She fired again, several shots in rapid succession, and two more cops bit the dust in the hail of lead. Mona was curiously unmoved by the carnage but was astonished at Terri's accomplished marksmanship.

Cullen studied the unattended motorcycle, then Travers, Jerry and the remaining deputies who were busy pumping bullets at Terri. He nudged Mona, gesturing at the bike.

He whispered, "There's our chance. It's a slim one, but –"

"I'm not leaving Terri."

"She's playing out her hand. You heard her. She wants you to go. And she's covering us."

"No."

"Mona, she's already dead"

"No."

"Yes, Mona. Now come on." He tugged at her arm. She quickly glanced at the shack, then Travers, then Cullen. All at once they were up-and-running to the motorcycle. Travers abruptly caught on. She turned, rising slightly as her remaining men fired at the cabin. She drew a bead on the running Mona. Just then, Terri shot off Travers' hat and, startled, Travers let off her bullet before she could steady her aim.

Cullen stopped in mid-flight, hit in the back. His knees crumpled, and he toppled backwards in the dust. Mona screamed, crouched, then propped herself on both arms over her fallen man. He looked helplessly up at her, blood already issuing in a narrow stream from his lips.

A look of horror spread across Travers' face as she realized she'd mortally wounded her ex-lover.

Cullen struggled to speak, "Keep going."

Mona sank lower towards him, tears welling up on her cheeks, then passionately kissed him on his bloodstained mouth. She held his face in both her hands as she mashed her lips against his, squeezing her eyes tightly shut. She pulled away as he tried to speak, her chin smeared scarlet.

The blasting of the guns became barely audible to her, like the muffled roar of cannons on a far distant battlefield.

"Goddamn it, honey, get out of here."

Mona shook her head, " No, no, I can't leave you."

Cullen could barely speak, "Damn it, Mona…you've been

the strongest one of all of us…right down the line…now get the fuck going!"

She tore herself away from him at last, rising and starting to run to the bike. Cullen tried to raise his head to watch her. Even though Travers had her hands full and was pinned down, she nevertheless had been jealously watching them, keeping tabs on Mona. When she saw her bolt for the cycle, she threw caution to the wind, stood and walked up besides Cullen. She aimed her gun at Mona with outstretched arms and squeezed off a shot, hitting Mona in the left calf just as she climbed onto the machine.

Terri took careful aim with the rifle.

"Travers," she whispered, "you fucking bitch!" She fired. Travers, hit in the back, fell forward onto the ground as Mona kick-started the motorcycle, and it roared to life.

Jerry and the remaining cops tried to take aim at Mona, but Terri unleashed a savage, renewed volley of lead, pinning them down. The dying Travers raised herself, aimed and fired again as Mona began to move. She was hit in the upper right shoulderblade, which caused her to swerve as she gained momentum.

Suddenly Cullen jumped from behind, collapsed on Travers' back and reached around with his right hand to jam her revolver up against her chest. He embraced her as he snaked his finger alongside hers in the trigger guard, then squeezed, firing point blank into her heart, and the bullet exploded out of her spine and up through him, too.

Terri slumped away from the window as she saw this. She stared into empty space as she zombie-like pulled the plunger detonator over to her. The boom box still roared away, and she dialed it even louder.

Terri mumbled to herself, "Jesus, let her get away."

She pressed the plunger down.

The two police cruisers and remaining deputies were poised directly over the mined area and suddenly disappeared in the massive explosion.

Mona screamed as she heard the eruption, still careening on the motorcycle, trying to keep control of the bulky machine. It was unlike any other cycle she'd ever ridden. She squeezed her eyes shut for a second at the sounds, then glanced backwards to see the flames blooming behind her. Then the shack exploded, too.

Tears streamed down Mona's bloodstreaked cheeks.

She wailed, eaten up with anguish and despair.
Travers' last shot had pierced her lungs.
A tiny stream of blood trickled between her lips.
She flew down the road beneath overhanging tree branches.
A raven sitting there was startled into flight, and it cawed
loudly as it followed her in the sky around the next bend in the road.

Chris D. is also author of the novels *NO EVIL STAR,
MOTHER'S WORRY, SHALLOW WATER* and the collection
*DRAGON WHEEL SPLENDOR AND OTHER LOVE STORIES OF VIOLENCE
AND DREAD*, all from Poison Fang Books. His anthology *A MINUTE
TO PRAY, A SECOND TO DIE*, a 500 page collection of selected
short stories, excerpts from novels and scores of dream journal
entries, as well as all of his poetry and song lyrics, was published in
December 2009 His non-fiction *OUTLAW MASTERS OF JAPANESE
FILM* was published by IB Tauris (distributed by Palgrave Macmil-
lan in the USA) in 2005. He saw release of his first feature film as
director, *I PASS FOR HUMAN*, in 2004 (and its DVD release in
2006), and worked as a programmer at The American Cinematheque
in Hollywood, California from 1999-2009. Chris D. is also known as
the singer/songwriter of the bands The Flesh Eaters, Divine Horsemen
and Stone by Stone. He was an A&R rep and in-house producer at
Slash Records/Ruby Records from 1980-1984.
April 2013 saw the release of his 800 page non-fiction *GUN AND
SWORD: AN ENCYCLOPEDIA OF JAPANESE GANGSTER FILMS 1955-1980*.
His latest are the novels *VOLCANO GIRLS* and *TIGHTROPE ON
FIRE*, from Poison Fang Books. Upcoming works include the novel,
*TATTOOED BLOOD.*.

**Thank yous** to Donna Lethal, Sylvie Simmons, Alan K. Rode, Byron Coley, Lili Dwight, Craig Owens, Wayne Valdez of Store 54, Peter Maravelis of City Lights, Gwen Deglise, Craig Clevenger, Eddie Muller, Taquila Mockingbird, Shepherd Stevenson, Richard Lange, Liz Garo & Alex Maslansky & Claudia Colodro of Stories, Billy Shire & Matt Kennedy of Wacko/La Luz de Jesus, Dan Kusunoki of Skylight Books, Curtis Tsui, Joey O'Brien, Liz Helfgott, John Roller, Tosh Berman of Tam Tam Books, Feeding Tube Records in Northampton, Other Music in Manhattan

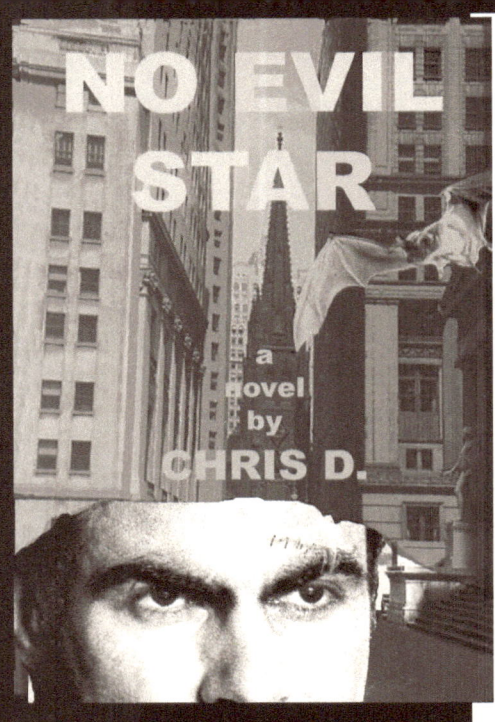

The life of recovering addict and Namvet Milo unravels when ex-CIA friend Dave goes off the deep end. Not only is Dave the heist man whacking NYC drug dealers, he's also hatching a scheme to plunder mob boss Nunzio's art treasures pilfered in WWII. Complicating matters, Yuen, an ex-Viet Cong with a grudge against Milo and Dave, arrives in New York.

"*A healthy authorial sense of curiosity and generosity lends weight to* No Evil Star*'s intersecting lives, where Chris D. ably traces out the contours of human torment in a manner recalling American films of the 1970s.*"
– Grace Krilanovich, author of THE ORANGE EATS CREEPS

# AVAILABLE NOW FROM POISON FANG BOOKS

In Chris D.'s title novella, brilliant, alcoholic Anne, unable to succeed in downtown L.A.'s arts community, helps a Japanese-American girl escape forced prostitution, only to ignite a string of violent deaths. In "The Glider," a British policewoman falls in-love with a serial killer near the white cliffs of Dover; plus five more twisted love tales.

"*...seems to shimmer with menace... with* DRAGON WHEEL SPLENDOR, *the great Chris D should finally find the audience he deserves...a book that can kill the voices in your head - or make you love them.*"
– Jerry Stahl, author of PLAINCLOTHES NAKED, PAINKILLERS and PERMANENT MIDNIGHT

DRAGON WHEEL SPLENDOR
and Other Love Stories of Violence and Dread

by Chris D.

"...shimmers with menace...the great Chris D. should finally find the audience he deserves..."
-- Jerry Stahl

The year is 1987, and outlaw Ray Diamond's mother is the queenpin of crime in Mystic, GA. After his Navy discharge, Ray knocks over a mob-connected El Paso liquor store, not counting on Eli, the owner's psycho son, dogging his trail. Back home in Mystic, Ray's girl, Connie Eustace, resorts to stripping at Mama Lorna's club to make ends meet. Witness to a murder by the local sheriff, she goes on a drug-and-drink bender, jumping from the frying pain into the fire.

*"...a crazy dive into a universe populated largely by monsters...a classic update of the Gold Medal/Lion Library loser noir tradition. Great work... "*
– Byron Coley, writer for WIRE magazine, author of C'EST LA GUERRE: EARLY WRITINGS 1978-1983

MOTHER'S WORRY

a novel by CHRIS D.

## FROM POISON FANG BOOKS   AVAILABLE NOW

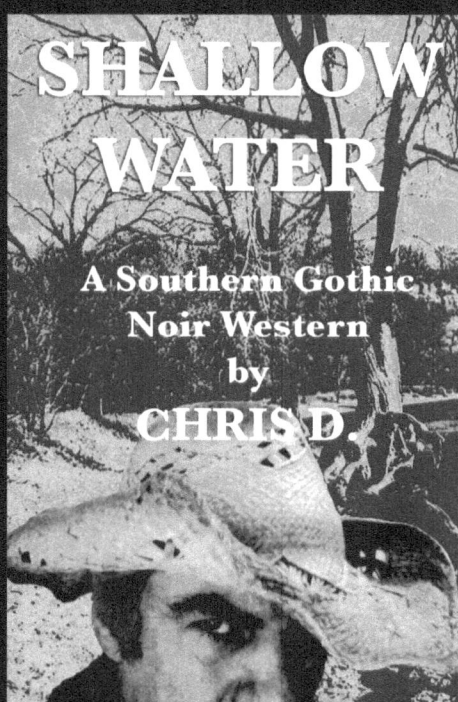

SHALLOW WATER

A Southern Gothic Noir Western by CHRIS D.

Post-Civil War, bitter rebel veteran and bounty hunter, Santo Brady, drifts through the Deep South. When he rescues halfbreed Indian prostitute, Lucy Damien, from one backwater town, he has the world fall in on his head. They embark on a freight-train-hopping odyssey to New Orleans, unaware that Lucy's rich white father and homicidal brother are tracking them. A tragic tall tale plunging head-first into a wild heart of darkness.

*"One sinsister serpent of a story, an old Republic Pictures western serial scripted by James M. Cain and reimagined by Sam Peckinpah. I loved it."*
– Eddie Muller, author of THE DISTANCE and SHADOW BOXER

# Two New Novels from Chris D.
# Available October 2013

Half-sisters, schoolteacher Mona and junkie punk rocker Terri, are uneasy roommates while taking care of their sick mother. When their boyfriends, cop Johnny Cullen and killer Merle Chambers, clash due to labor struggles in their small town of Devil's River, the two women are pulled into the fray. To make matters worse, jealous female sheriff, Billie Travers, decides Mona is intruding on her faltering love affair, and quiet small town life amps up into an apocalyptic nightmare of uncontrollable violence and destruction.

Corrupt female police detective, Frankie Powers, is treading water in her small desert hometown of Sweet Home, California. Burned-out and emotionally numb after losing her husband and child in a mysterious fire ten years before, her conscience is reawakened when her affair with a Bakersfield narc brings new facts to light. Frankie's mob boss uncle, Jack Richman, has been kidnapping under-age girls for his Vegas prostitution syndicate; he's also been victimizing his own teen daughters, Frankie's twin bad girl cousins, Valerie and Vanessa. Soon Frankie finds herself singlehand-edly fighting tooth-and-nail against not only wicked uncle Jack but also his dominatrix wife, Marilyn and their degenerate hitman, Cal Nero. Can a lone shewolf survive against the bloodthirsty pack?

from **P**oison **F**ang **B**ooks